Green Horse Winter

Isolde Pullum

Green Horse Winter

Copyright © 2004 by Isolde Pullum
Original title: Green Horse Winter
Cover ill: © 2003 Jennifer Bell
Cover layout: Stabenfeldt AS
Published by PonyClub, Stabenfeldt AS
Edited by Karen Pasacreta
Printing: GGP Media, Germany 2004

ISBN: 82-591-1136-5

Chapter one

"Mail," called Dave Wells to his daughter. "Looks like there are some cards for you."

Jenna mumbled something unintelligible from the top of the stepladder where she was putting up brightly colored foil Christmas decorations in the hallway. She held the tape between her teeth as she stretched her arm up to the high ceiling to reach the final dusty corner.

Carefully she came down the ladder, her long, thin legs looking even longer in her old, blue riding pants with her toes poking out of the end of her socks. At this moment, with cobwebs in her hair, she looked much younger than her 15 years, especially when she pushed her feet into her mother's fluffy pink slippers, which were too large for her. At other times, when she fussed over her clothes and wore her dark hair loose instead of in a ponytail, she could pass for 17, though Jenna was completely unaware of this.

"It looks lovely, Jen, very festive," her father told her as they both admired the entrance to their hotel, bedecked with gold and silver streamers, glittery baubles, and a large tree complete with lights and a fairy.

Jenna picked up her cards from the front desk and went to the kitchen to fix herself a hot chocolate. She felt a shiver of excitement run through her as she thought about the holiday ahead of her. School had just let out for winter break, so for the first time in weeks she'd have time to ride every day and hopefully make some improvement with Gold's show jumping. There was an indoor show she wanted to go to — that is if she could persuade her father to let her. On top of all that, this was their first Christmas as proprietors of the Green Horse Hotel and, to add to the festive spirit, they were holding a themed event.

Back in autumn when Dave, Angie, and Jenna had discussed the possibility of holding a "Murder Mystery Weekend" over the Christmas break it seemed like a great idea. A company had been hired to manage the event, and Dave and Angie had started taking reservations immediately. They had done all the necessary planning to ensure that the weekend was extra special. The idea was for the guests to take part in solving a "murder" that would take place in the hotel, played out by a professional cast of actors that would mingle with the guests. Jenna was taking part, as well as helping in the restaurant and, best of all, her friends Alice and James had persuaded their parents to have their family Christmas at the Green Horse hotel.

Sipping her hot chocolate at the long farm table in the kitchen, Jenna began to open her cards as her mother Angie, put yet another huge tray of bread rolls into the large, stainless steel oven. There were two cards from friends she used to know in London, one with a silver star from Tiffany and one, which spilled glitter into her lap, from a girl called Jessica who Jenna had never really liked. A pang of guilt crept over her as she realized how little she had thought of her city friends since she had moved to the country.

"Have you got any spare cards?" she asked her mother as she opened a third envelope.

"There might be a few in the office," Angie replied, coming to look over Jenna's shoulder. "Who's that one from?"

"It doesn't say." Jenna turned the card over and then picked up the envelope again. "It's a local postmark. The address is typed, and I don't recognize the handwriting."

The message, written in red ink, was simple: "Jenna – if you can, have a HAPPY Christmas." The words seemed to shout at her from the card.

"What an odd thing to write," said her mother, looking over Jenna's shoulder. "It's not signed either. I expect whoever it was got distracted when they were writing it; it's only half of a message.

Well, that isn't an uncommon mistake, especially if you're writing lots of them at the same time."

"Yes," said Jenna quietly, "You're probably right." But there was something a bit creepy about the unsigned card which made Jenna uneasy. Instead of putting it on the dresser with her other cards, she slipped it into the trash when her mother wasn't looking.

***

After the lunchtime rush Jenna was able to run down to the stables, happy to be free of her black, waitress's uniform and more comfortably dressed in riding pants, short boots, and half chaps. Her blue fleece, zipped up to the neck, was too warm for the mild, winter weather they were having and Jenna sweated a bit as she skipped out Gold's stable box. Gold's stall was next to Steve's two young thoroughbreds, Spiral and Gizelle. Steve hoped to make a name for himself as a race horse trainer, and he rented the once grand stable yard from Jenna's dad. It had been neglected over the years but he liked its faded elegance that hinted at a more decorative age. It wasn't ideal because it lacked the modern conveniences Steve had been used to at his father's successful training yard, but it was all Steve could afford, and he was grateful for the independence it gave him. Things were going well for Steve, it had been a spectacular season so far with Spiral winning both her races and Gizelle coming third in one of hers, amply repaying the trust that Steve's father had put in him when he'd let Steve train her. One of the boxes was empty, and that meant Steve was out on Spiral. If Jenna was lucky he'd be back soon and able to help her to school Gold in the paddock, where they had marked out an arena. Although Jenna saw Steve most days, the thought of him still sent a little shiver through her – kind of like butterflies. He was very good looking and would have turned the head of any young girl, but Jenna knew there was a bit more to it than that. She liked the way he talked to her, the way he took time to explain things, and the way he consulted her when he was unsure about something. She liked his unruly, wavy dark hair and his pale, sparkling eyes, and the way he was always on a diet in case he got too heavy to ride his beloved horses. He was the only man she'd ever met who knew the calorie content of a banana or a slice of toast, or even a chocolate bar. Most of all she liked the way he sometimes glanced at her sideways when she wasn't supposed to see, but she recognized in that look some of her own feelings and was confused by them. She thought of him as she swept clean shavings back into the box and, as if by magic, he appeared through the red brick archway that was the entrance to the stables. Gold whickered gently to Gizelle, who ignored him as she walked purposefully towards her full rack of hay.

"Hi Jen," Steve called, "I'm just about to take Spiral out if you want to come with me."

Bliss! thought Jenna, an hour trotting through the lanes with Steve for company. Then she remembered her plans for schooling.

"I ought to jump Gold today, I'm taking him to the riding club show tomorrow and the Talent Spotters competition is straight after Christmas…he still can't canter into a fence slowly!"

"That's what too much galloping as a youngster does for a horse, it's a big problem when they've been in race training." Steve wasn't telling her anything she didn't already know. "I tell you what, you hack out with me, and I'll put some jumps up for you when we come back. He might settle better if he's not so fresh."

Double bliss! Jenna was in her element as the two of them set off down the drive towards the village. She sat tall in the soft, black leather saddle that she'd bought second hand with what remained of the money from the sale of some driving harness that had been discovered in the closed off attic of the stables. After she'd paid for Gold there wasn't much left, but a proper jumping saddle had been important and it was a pleasant change from the flat, racing one she'd been used to riding him in when he'd belonged to Steve. Before Steve had brought Gold and Spiral to the yard, Jenna had only had Tufty to ride, he had been left at the hotel by his previous owners and was too old for hard work. However, there would always be a place in her heart for the old pony, who now enjoyed a restful retirement in one of the paddocks at the Green Horse Hotel. Jenna still couldn't quite believe that Gold was really hers, as only a few months before, owning him had seemed an impossible dream. Now she had full responsibility for his schooling and training, and more than anything she wanted to jump; she thought about it morning, noon, and night. She could hardly wait for the season to begin. Jenna wanted to become a professional show jumper if she turned out to be good enough, and somehow, she knew that she could be. She was aiming for the prestigious Talent Spotters Competition that was held in a big equestrian center a few miles away. The prize for winning that was training with top show jumper Harry Houseman, and an opportunity to compete with a professional young rider's team. Jenna wanted that very badly indeed and, without loads of money behind her, it seemed the only way in to the elusive and seemingly glamorous world of top class show jumping. The show she hoped to attend on the following day would be a very different matter, but Jenna knew that all practice was very good for them. If her dad let her, she would ride the eight miles to Trent Hall, a rather small indoor school where the local riding club were holding their Christmas show. The roads would be busy and the daylight hours short. She knew her father wasn't keen on her going alone, but Steve was racing and the hotel was at its busiest, so there was no alternative.

As they rode through the village Jenna waved to

old Mr. Penrose who sat by his window and watched the world go by.

"It must be cold," Steve turned to her, "if Mr. Penrose isn't out in his garden."

"He doesn't spend so much time out as he used to, not since he was ill. It's a shame really, I like talking to him."

"That's not what you used to tell me. You said he used to scare you with all his tales of ghostly green horses up at your place."

"Well, perhaps he did like to be a bit mysterious, but I'm quite fond of him really," Jenna replied remembering how attached the old man was to Tufty, who he'd looked after during the years when he worked at the hotel.

The day was sunny, but dark clouds were gathering over the hillside as the two horses and their silent riders cantered up a muddy track leading away from the village.

Steve was 20 and very independent. He had had to grow up quickly during the past few years when rows with his explosive father, the successful race horse trainer Eric Lambert, had forced him to leave home and start up by himself. Although they were currently reconciled, Steve knew it wouldn't take very much for things to go bad between them again, and he liked to keep his independence whenever possible. The set-up at Jenna's was perfect and he was grateful to Dave Wells for letting him rent the stable yard cheaply while he was establishing himself. The only disconcerting thing was Jenna, who he was growing more and more fond of. It was only in the way he'd be fond of a little sister, he kept telling himself, but sometimes, when she gave him one of her special looks, he wasn't so sure. She made him laugh and she was good to talk things over with, but she was really just a kid. They cantered on and Steve looked behind him as the wind tore tears from his eyes and he could see her beautiful face grinning with pure delight at the speed of her horse. Yes, she's just a nice kid, he told himself.

Half an hour later he was shouting at Jenna as she tore into fence after fence without the least little bit of control over Gold, whose head was sky-high with excitement.

"Get your legs on him, ride him, don't let him cart you about like that," he shouted in frustration, desperate to get on Gold himself, but knowing from experience that Jenna had to do it for herself.

"I have got my legs on!" Jenna was close to tears. "He doesn't seem to notice."

She circled Gold at the top of the paddock and managed to get him a little more in control. Tentatively she rode him into a fence, a small upright made of oil drums. Three strides away Gold took hold and shot towards the fence like the steeplechaser he had once been. He met it low and flat, and the flimsy pole wrapped around his front legs and snapped in two on landing.

"I think we're going to have to go right back to

poles on the ground and work him up gently," said Steve, more kindly now he'd seen Jenna's tear-stained face.

"What about the competition?" she asked.

"Well, we could try a stronger bit if you're determined to enter him, though it's not really the answer, if it works at all it will probably only be a temporary fix. Schooling is the only long-term solution, masses of schooling and grids and pole work until he's like clockwork and doesn't run away from you."

"When am I going to get time to do it?" asked Jenna, suddenly feeling helpless and weighed down with responsibility. "I've promised to help out over Christmas and the days are so short at this time of the year."

"I've got some news about Christmas," said Steve. "My Dad's treating the whole family to your crazy Murder Mystery weekend. I've been summoned to join in the fun whether I like it or not! Some friends of his booked ages ago, and they've just persuaded him to bag the last few places, so it will be a bit of a Lambert take-over, I'm afraid. We're a noisy bunch when we get together."

Jenna was immediately excited by the news. The idea of having Steve around, actually taking part in the fun that was going to happen at the hotel, made the thought of all the work it would involve seem more enjoyable.

"Good," she said to him, with one of her golden smiles made even more endearing through slightly tear-dampened lashes. "Perhaps we'll get time for schooling Gold on Christmas morning!"

Steve grinned at her, charmed by her enthusiasm, but he shook his head.

" Much as I'd love to stand around in a muddy field shouting at you, I expect I shall be far too busy solving murders!" he said in a mock pompous voice.

Jenna started to laugh, and with Gold's awful jumping temporarily forgotten they led him back to the stables together. Jenna suddenly realized that she was looking very much forward to Christmas.

Jenna usually got her own way if she was clever about it, and she wasn't really surprised to find herself trotting along the wide, busy road that led to the far side of Tuxford and on to Trent Hall, the venue for the riding club show. She looked very smart in her dark blue riding coat, polished boots, and almost clean jodhpurs; there was a small smear of hoof oil across her right knee, but luckily only she could see it. Steve had left hours before them in a hired horse lorry, heading for the next county and a small race meeting. Usually Jenna would go with him as groom and she'd been torn between the enjoyment of a day out with Steve and knowing that she desperately needed more practice. Gold was unconcerned as the cars whizzed past them, their wheels hissing on the wet road and splashing his white legs. It had stopped raining and the sun was making its best effort to shine. Jenna checked her watch, it would only take an hour to get there, and she wanted to ride in the first two classes, which were especially for novice horses and their riders.

Jenna found the riding school easily. The car park was already filling up with lorries and cars pulling trailers and horses with rugs, protective boots, and tail bandages were being led down ramps and tied up to rings on the sides of their vehicles. The young ones tugged at their ropes and tried to turn round to look at everything at once, but the older, more experienced horses stood quietly and pulled at hay nets, calmly awaiting their moment of glory. Jenna cursed herself for not thinking of bringing a headcollar and wondered if she dared ask someone to lend her one. She dismounted and led Gold to a caravan where two elderly ladies were sitting inside taking entries through the open window. They were getting very flustered as they seemed to have a lot of papers, which kept blowing off the table. Jenna tried not to laugh as she paid her money, told them her name and took her number, which she tied around her waist with a long, black tape.

"I think they're already walking the course for class one, dear," the old lady told her, "you'd better hurry up."

Jenna rushed over to the entrance of the indoor school and then another thought struck her. She couldn't take Gold into the school to look at the jumps, it wasn't allowed, but neither could she leave him wandering about outside by himself. Luckily, a man who was standing nearby holding a dark bay horse understood her problem.

"Would you like me to look after him for you?" he asked her. "I'm holding my daughter's horse while she walks the course, one more won't hurt."

"Oh, would you, thanks ever so much," she replied and, handing him the reins, she rushed into the school.

The jumps were smaller than Jenna had hoped for, and she knew that Gold might not take them seriously. The school was small and the track twisted and wound around it making it hard for Jenna to learn the course. The jumps themselves shouldn't be a problem, she thought, but controlling Gold in this tight space will be. Giving it one last look, Jenna wrote her number on the chalkboard and went back to collect Gold from the friendly man. His daughter was already mounted on her tall, bay gelding.

"What do you think of the course?" she asked Jenna with a cheerful grin.

"Bit twisty for my horse. He can get rather enthusiastic sometimes," Jenna told her. "How about yours?"

"It's his first show, so I'm not expecting much, we're just here for the experience."

They chatted away for a while and then Jenna realized that her number was getting near the top of the list, so she went to find a practice fence.

Jenna had thought the main arena was small, but the warm-up area was tiny. On top of that, it was full of horses and nervous-looking riders trotting aimlessly in circles and taking it in turns to jump over a pole hung across two barrels. She stood at the entrance and wondered if she dared go in. It was bedlam in there; the riders weren't even going in the same direction and Jenna thought it was only a matter of time before someone got kicked. She turned Gold and they went back and stood by the arena door.

"You're next to go, I think," said the woman in charge.

Jenna started feeling butterflies tickling inside her stomach as she realized how unprepared she and Gold were. At home she knew he would jump just about anything she asked him to, but it was always the lack of control in between the fences that let them down. The woman pulled the big rolling doors back, and a young man on a skewbald cob came through them; he was patting and praising his horse and they both looked flushed with exertion.

Jenna asked Gold to walk on and they entered the indoor school cautiously. Inside, the air was stuffy and dust swirled in the light streaming through the gaps in the walls. Gold snorted and it echoed back to them and made him jump. Jenna pushed him into a trot and, as they circled the school, he shied at the fences and picked up his feet in an exaggerated manner as they thumped down with a hollow echo on the compacted, earthy surface. The bell went and Jenna pointed Gold towards the first fence, which he jumped so high that he had to skip half a stride to twist himself over the second that seemed to come upon them suddenly. Across the school they jumped a wall and a spread of white poles and Gold bounded on, getting stronger and braver with every stride. It was when they were riding up the center line, still over-jumping the tiny obstacles, that Gold suddenly caught sight of his reflection in the large, grimy mirror ahead. He stopped dead and Jenna flew over his head, holding firmly on to the reins and taking his bridle with her. Finding himself loose and bridleless in a strange arena, Gold felt very special. He raised himself up to his full height and passaged round the school doing the most wonderfully slow, elevated trot, scooting away when anyone came near him and evading capture for several minutes. Jenna, crimson with embarrassment, couldn't help but admire him, while at the same time cursing him, as she listened to the laughter coming from the gallery. When Gold tired of his game he allowed himself to be caught, and Jenna found herself outside in the cold once more, dusty, bruised, and defeated. She bought herself some chocolate and wouldn't give Gold any, which made her feel slightly better.

"You are a stupid animal," she told him, more affectionately now that she was beginning to see the funny side of what had happened. "Did you think there was a big, ugly chestnut horse in there about to get you?"

Their second round wasn't much of an improvement, though, as Jenna told herself later, at least she didn't fall off. Their canter had quickly become a gallop, and Jenna could do little more than hang on and try to make the tight, twisting turns without actually falling over. Miraculously they had a clear round, but Jenna excused herself from the jump-off when she passed the judge on the way out.

"I think that's wise, dear," he'd said, "a bit more schooling needed before you take him against the clock!"

"A bit more something, I just wish I knew *what*," Jenna muttered to herself as she slipped away quietly and began the ride home, wondering how she was going to learn to control her glorious golden horse, whom she loved dearly in spite of the heartache he caused her. As the light of the short winter day began to fade, her spirits faded with it, and she seemed a million miles away from her dream of becoming a successful, professional show jumper.

It was dark when Jenna went to see Tufty after she'd settled Gold in for the night. He was waiting restlessly for her at the gate, circling and calling, his little brown and white ears pricked and listening for her footsteps. He hardly seemed to know what to do with himself these days; as soon as Jenna put him out, he was anxious to come in again, but when he was in, he couldn't wait to go out. It was all very odd. Jenna rubbed his face and smoothed his thick, coarse mane over to the proper side and watched, amused, as it sprang back.

"Scruff," she said fondly, buckling his headcollar

and leading him back to the stables. His box was one of the old coach houses to the side of the main building. It was dark and shadowy, ancient and a little bit ramshackle and it was always at this time, the strange ageless period between day and night that Jenna most felt the weighty atmosphere that seemed to be part of the fabric of the building. She gave Tufty his feed and watched awhile, pained by the realization that he was getting thinner, gaunt, and more angular about the hips, despite a thick padding of winter coat to disguise it. He was very, very old. No one quite knew how old but Mr. Penrose guessed at thirty. Jenna fetched another scoop of feed from the bin in the tack room, and Tufty buried his head in the bucket and ate with silent satisfaction.

Chapter two

The next morning, after breakfast had been served
and cleared away, Jenna was called into her father's
office to meet Michael McCauley, the director and
writer of the Murder Mystery event. Dave Wells had
been working closely with Michael for several
weeks and many faxes and emails had been exchanged about the storyline. As the plot was devel-
oped, the Wells family had been able to make several suggestions, some of which had been used to tai-
lor the event to the Green Horse Hotel. It had become a historical drama, and the guests had all been
invited to enter into the spirit of the occasion and
come in costume. Jenna was a little shy at first. She
sat on the edge of the green leather sofa and sipped
her tea, listening intently but not contributing to the
conversation. Michael, his curly hair still damp from
an early swim in the hotel's new pool, was outlining
the plot, which he'd based on a true story he'd discovered when looking through some old ledgers and
court documents Dave had unearthed in the hotel's

attic. From this scant information, Michael had pieced together a complicated tale, involving a wager between twin brothers, Arnold and Abram, who argue over their uncle's will. The two agree to ride against each other in a dangerous, moonlit steeplechase to decide who will inherit the hotel – at the time a prosperous coaching inn. After the race, the victorious brother, Arnold, is found in the coach house, shot dead and Abram is accused of his murder. According to the documents Abram denied killing his brother, but he disappeared before he was tried and his absence was considered proof of his guilt. The mystery was never solved and the people of the village were divided by their separate loyalties. Michael elaborated on the story and invented other people who might have wanted Arnold dead, weaving dark secrets and lies into the plot, which the guests would have to decipher in order to solve the mystery.

Listening in silence, Jenna's head began to spin long before Michael had finished. If she didn't understand it when she knew the whole story, she couldn't imagine what the guests would make of it from a series of clues and red herrings. All she could think of was what Mr. Penrose would say about them acting out one of the hotel's grizzly episodes from the past; he could be a bit funny about things like that.

"When are the actors arriving?" asked Angie, appearing with a fresh pot of coffee.

She perched on the arm of the settee where Jenna

sat, and exchanged a grin with her daughter. Angie was in her element with a hotel full of guests and the excitement of Christmas upon her. Tall, dark haired, and slim, she was dazzling even in her apron and with flour on her cheek.

"Tomorrow morning. We'll spend the day working through the script. We'll need a private room," Michael told her.

"Have you worked together before?" Dave asked.

"Oh yes, many times. I tend to use the same actors. I know I can trust them to improvise should the plot get a bit lost – it can happen sometimes, and you need experienced people who you know will react appropriately."

"What about the ones who get murdered?" Jenna asked.

"The first one just leaves quietly on Christmas Eve and goes home to have turkey with his wife and children, the second has to make a quick getaway after lunch on Boxing Day" Michael told her.

"Hopefully no guests will spot them leaving!" said Jenna, amused at the idea of a walking corpse. A thought crossed her mind, "Are you going to have real horses for the race?"

"No, too much to organize without hiring a couple of racehorses and stunt doubles for my non-horsy actors." Michael paused thoughtfully. "Why, are you offering? It would make a fantastic spectacle for the guests if we could put on a horse race for them after dinner."

"Sounds dangerous," said Dave, "with loads of horses careering about in the dark."

"Only two," said Jenna, "and we only need to canter across the lawn where it's floodlit and get the guests to watch from the steps. I bet Steve would be up for it."

Jenna's mind began to work overtime. What a thrill it would be to gallop after dark dressed up as a man in the clothes of another century. Better still, she'd have Steve with her to share in the excitement.

"Do you think you could do it?" asked Michael, deliberately avoiding the look that Dave Wells was giving him. "It would certainly be the highlight of the evening – fantastically authentic – far better than the coconut shells I was going to use!"

"I think it's too dangerous," her Dad said again. "What do you think, Angie?"

"Well, it would look wonderful, but I'd never forgive myself if anything happened."

"Oh please, I know it would be all right – Gold's quite sensible most of the time and, if Steve agrees, then you can be sure he'll look after me."

"Well, maybe, if Steve thinks he can make it safe," said Dave, realizing what a spectacle it would be for the guests.

"That's settled then." Jenna jumped up, fired with the excitement of adventure. I'm going to find Steve and tell him the good news."

To Jenna's disappointment, Steve wasn't in the yard. His battered sports car was missing too, so she turned her attention to Gold, who had not had a thorough grooming in some time.

She relished the warming work of brushing his dusty coat and seeing the shine return to the rich, chestnut hairs. Gold stopped pulling at his hay and sighed with contentment. Being groomed was one of his favorite pastimes, and his lower lip began to droop as Jenna's brushing had its usual, soporific effect on him. Outside it began to rain, lashing the thick walls of the stable and pattering against the windows. Jenna fetched an exercise rug, which she placed under the saddle, covering the thin-skinned thoroughbred's back and quarters. She led Gold into the yard to mount, and he turned his back to the wind and bucked slightly as she got on.

The rain was coming down in sheets, which seemed to wrap around Jenna as she trotted briskly down the lane leading away from the stable yard. Gold's head was held low in his efforts to keep the water from his eyes and soon Jenna could feel the icy rain penetrating her jacket and running down her neck. She shivered involuntarily and urged Gold forward, heading towards the stony track that would lead them, at a canter, towards Wisely Plantation.

"Just once round the woods. You'll like it when we get there," Jenna told the chestnut thoroughbred, as she leaned forward and patted his streaming neck.

At nearly 16 hands and only 5 years old, he was about as much horse as Jenna could handle.

Gold slipped on some wet leaves as the pair entered the woods, and Jenna had to concentrate hard, steering the powerful chestnut towards a line of low, brushwood jumps, keeping him firmly between her hands and legs as she struggled to control his speed. The trees shot past them in a blur of late autumn colors made gray by falling rain. All cold and discomfort were forgotten as the adrenaline kicked in and Jenna's spirits soared, in a rush of speed and delicious fear. She felt more alive than she'd ever felt before, with the cold and the rain scorching her face and the soft thundery sound of muffled hoof beats echoing through her body.

The accident happened within the blink of an eye. Gold lost his feet on a muddy corner and, as he sprawled and paddled and fought to regain his balance, Jenna shot off sideways and skidded gracelessly through the wet leaf mould, rolling and tumbling, bruised and winded. For a while she lay on her back staring at the gray sky through the canopy of naked winter branches, which swam in and out of focus. Vaguely she wondered what Gold was doing, but when she raised her head to look she saw him nonchalantly nibbling at the shoots of a chestnut tree. Gratefully, she sank back down again, closed her eyes, and listened to the noises of the wood. It all seemed very peaceful now after the roaring wind of her headlong gallop, with just the sounds of water dripping on to sodden ground, a Robin's shrill, piercing notes and Gold's rhythmical crunching. Jenna lay there for a while until cold made her sit up and gingerly test her limbs. Apart from aching all over, she seemed none the worse for wear, though her legs felt like jelly as she mounted Gold. They were a more subdued pair who walked and trotted carefully home.

Back at the stables, Steve waited anxiously as the premature dark of a stormy day settled around him. He swept the yard fiercely, pushing piles of dead leaves, mixed with water, across the cobbles. Why did Jenna insist on going out in all weathers? he kept asking himself, and at this time of the day too. When he heard the sound of hooves trotting fast over tarmac he heaved a sigh of relief and went quickly back to the tack room to make up the evening feeds, anxious that Jenna shouldn't know he'd been looking out for her.

Despite being bruised and battered and soaked to the skin, Jenna felt happy when she returned to the yard. It looked welcoming and familiar; Steve's car was back in its usual place and the lights were glowing warmly through the small panes of thin glass that made up the ancient windows. She could hear the familiar noises of the evening feeds being made up, of buckets being filled, hooves scraping on the cobbles, and Spiral calling impatiently to Steve to hurry before she starved to death. Jenna led Gold in through the double-doored entrance and into his box where she replaced his tack with a warm, lightweight stable rug while he buried his delicate, thoroughbred head in his manger and ate. Steve appeared in the doorway.

"I heard you racing back. How many times do I have to tell you to walk the last mile?" he asked her, unable to suppress his annoyance. "You're going to ruin his legs."

"You try making him walk when he's soaking wet and wants his food," Jenna replied.

"What on earth happened to you?" said Steve suddenly, alarmed to see Jenna so pale and covered in mud. A long scratch down her cheek had bled a little, and Steve was disconcerted when he realized he wanted to pick her up in his arms and soothe away the hurt.

Jenna grinned through the mud, not totally unaware of the effect she sometimes had on him.

"Gold slipped over in the woods, and I went out the side door! I'm all right, just a bit battered. He's OK too. I've checked him over and he doesn't seem to have a scratch on him."

"Were you galloping him in the woods?" Steve asked sternly.

"Well, maybe a fast canter." Jenna avoided looking at Steve, knowing he wouldn't believe her. "He's really hard to stop when he gets going."

"That's precisely why you shouldn't let him get going, not by yourself, anyway."

"I suppose now wouldn't be a good time to ask a favor of you?" said Jenna, hoping that her sad, muddy state might have a softening effect on Steve.

Steve gave her a questioning look through a furrowed brow.

"Dad and Michael want us to act out the moonlit steeplechase bit for the Murder Mystery... it would just be a bit of a canter across the lawn where the floodlights are," she said hurriedly, noticing his alarmed expression. "Just me on Gold and you on Gizelle, dressed up a bit..." her voice petered out when she found it hard to read his expression.

"I'll think about it," Steve said, turning away to hide a smile.

"Oh, brilliant, I knew you'd be up for it! I'll go and tell Michael."

***

"Phone call, darling." Angie's voice met Jenna's ears as soon as she came in through the back door. "It's the phone at the front desk – could you remind your friends not to call on that number in future?"

"Yes, Mum." Jenna kicked off her muddy boots at the door and padded through the passageway to reception.

She picked up the receiver from where it lay expectantly on top of a pile of hotel brochures.

"Hi," Jenna said. "It's Jenna, who's calling?"

The silence that answered her was full of atmosphere, not the empty deadness of a failed line.

"Hello," Jenna tried again. "Hello, who's there?"

Jenna waited a few seconds before trying again; she felt sure she could hear the strains of a distant radio behind the silent caller.

"Suit yourself," she said at last, feeling stupid for hanging on so long. Replacing the receiver she went thoughtfully back to find her mother.

"Who was it that wanted me?" she asked Angie when she found her.

"A woman, youngish, she sounded nice, but I didn't recognize her voice. When I asked who she was she seemed not to hear, so I didn't press it. Why are you asking?"

"No reason, it's just that we got cut off before she said what she wanted." Jenna wondered why she didn't tell her mother the whole story.

"Why don't you use the call back feature?" her mother asked. "If you're quick before another call comes in, then you could ring her back and find out."

"That's a good idea," Jenna raced back to the office, but before she even got there she could hear the phone ringing and her father's voice answering, in his official, friendly host way, the call which would cancel her mystery number out.

Chapter three

The late afternoon darkness was almost complete as Jenna pulled her bedroom curtains. It was the night before Christmas Eve and time for Jenna to get changed into her waitress's uniform to help her parents at the cheese and wine party that heralded the beginning of the festive celebrations.

"Why are the days so horribly short?" she spoke aloud, although she was alone in the room.

She sat in front of the decoratively carved mirror and stared at her reflection, not liking what she saw. The face that looked back was round and pretty with dark eyes and clear skin – that was OK- but what could she do to make herself look older?

"It's hardly surprising Steve's not interested in me," she moaned, "he doesn't want to be accused of robbing the cradle."

Jenna searched through a drawer for the few pieces of makeup she owned. She started with some brown eye shadow, which she applied rather inexpertly to her lids. The mascara was drying up and left black blobs on her already long, luxurious lashes. The blobs quickly transferred to her face, and she rubbed at them furiously, smudging them gray and reddening her sensitive skin. The lipstick was definitely a mistake. It was too dark and red for her pale complexion, and it drew the color from her face and made her look strange and ill. Sighing heavily, she reached for a bottle of cleanser which she smeared all over her face, mixing the red and the black and the brown across her cheeks and nose until her whole face was covered in a muddy, greasy film. She grinned and her teeth shone white through the gloom of the strange, masked face that stared at her from the mirror.

Ten minutes later, Jenna appeared in the hotel kitchen looking smart in her dark pinafore dress and white blouse. Her face glowed a little red from scrubbing, but that didn't hide her naturally good complexion or detract from her startlingly pretty eyes. Her mother looked up briefly from the tray of appetizers she was busily constructing and smiled at her daughter.

"You look lovely, darling. James won't be able to keep his eyes off you!" she said aloud. In her head she added, "and he won't be the only one!" Jenna's feelings for Steve had not gone unnoticed by Angie, and she'd also noticed the looks that Steve sometimes gave Jenna. It didn't worry her, she could remember having crushes on older boys when she was Jenna's age. She also remembered the heartache it had caused her and sighed for Jenna, but she knew there was nothing she could do to stop it; she'd just have to be there to pick up the pieces afterwards. Thankfully, James and Alice were due to arrive any time and Angie knew Jenna was looking forward to seeing them both. She hoped James would take Jenna's mind off Steve.

"Right then, these are finished. Can you take them through to the lounge and then come back for those other trays?" She pointed vaguely towards the pantry, her mind already firmly on the preparations for the evening meal.

For the next hour Jenna was rushed off her feet arranging food on the big lounge table, polishing glasses, and rolling napkins into interesting shapes that she was trying to copy from a book that belonged to her mother. She wasn't very good at this and some looked more interesting than skillful. It was while she was trying a particularly tricky swan and wishing she'd practiced more that James and Alice rushed into the room, wearing evening clothes, looking as if they'd just stepped from the pages of a society magazine, and carrying beautifully wrapped parcels. Jenna hugged them both, delighted to see them, but also aware of how glamorous they looked compared to her in her plain uniform. James kissed her on both cheeks and blushed a little because Jenna always had that effect on him. He looked almost grown up, Jenna thought, a bit like his dad in his dark suit with a brightly colored tie.

Alice was the same age as Jenna, but looked about 18; her blonde hair had been cut very short in a style that really suited her and her long, red dress accentuated her developing figure.

"This is for you." James held out a large, square parcel wrapped in gold paper and decorated with masses of curly ribbons.

"He wrapped it himself," Alice said in a teasing voice, "chose the paper and everything!"

Carefully Jenna removed the paper and opened the stout cardboard box. Inside there was a very handsome teddy bear, the expensive kind that wear hand-stitched clothes and have labels in their ears.

"Oh, isn't he gorgeous!" Jenna was genuinely delighted, "What's he called?"

"Call him James and cuddle up to him at night," said Alice.

James blushed and looked daggers at his sister.

"What's your second name?" Jenna asked James.

"It's Arthur," said Alice before James could reply.

"No it isn't!" James exploded.

"Isn't it? I think I'll call him Arthur anyway. No, Elegant Arthur, because he looks so smart in that waistcoat. Thank you ever so much. I'll give you your presents later."

"This is from me." Alice gave Jenna a blue and purple package tied with gold ribbon.

Inside Jenna found a set of her favorite soaps and a make-up kit.

"Oh, thanks, Alice, I could do with some new

make-up." Not to mention some advice as to how to use it, she thought ruefully to herself. "And I love the smell of this soap."

"I remembered; I like it too." Alice beamed at her. "And it covers up the smell of horses when you haven't time to shower!"

"Jenna," Angie's voice was calling from the kitchen, "I need you!"

"I hope you don't have to work all the time, you need to have a bit of time to yourself," James said.

"I'll have to do my bit, but Mum's hired a few extra people to help, so I should be able to have some fun too. Oh, and there's the steeplechase tomorrow, of course, I'm really looking forward to that."

Jenna heard loud, happy voices in the reception as she raced down the hallway with Elegant Arthur in one hand and the soaps in the other. She passed her father, who raised his eyebrows at the bear.

"Who's your friend?" he asked Jenna.

Grinning, but not bothering to reply, Jenna breezed into the kitchen, suddenly fired up by the spirit of Christmas and the warmth she felt for her friends and family. She stowed Arthur safely on top of a tall cupboard with the soaps and gathered another tray of glasses to take to the dining room. Softly she sang "Silent Night" to herself and allowed herself to daydream about who she'd like to be kissed by under the mistletoe. She set the tray down on the edge of an already overburdened side table.

"You've got a sweet voice, you ought to sing

more often." Steve's voice was warm and rich, but so unexpected that Jenna almost dropped the tray.

"You made me jump, you idiot! When did you arrive?" Jenna was aware she was blushing and couldn't decide whether it was because Steve had caught her singing or because he'd materialized when she'd been thinking about kissing him under the mistletoe.

"A few minutes ago – your dad said I'd find you in here. I wanted to give you this before the evening gets too hectic." He held out a dark green carrier bag bearing the name of the local saddlers in gold letters. "Sorry I didn't have time to wrap it," he added.

A little shot of anticipation went through Jenna as she felt the weight of the bag and her fingers recognized the strappy, slippery feel of leather through the thick plastic. She reached inside and the clean, oily smell of tanning wax and dyes escaped as she pulled out a beautiful, hand-stitched bridle. She was speechless as she felt the supple, pale leather and studied the shining snaffle bit connected to a pair of expensive, extra grippy reins of the sort Steve favored for racing.

"Thank you so, so much." She turned to him and couldn't help herself as she flung her arms around his neck and buried her face against the smooth cloth of his suit jacket, savoring the smell of his aftershave and wishing the moment could go on forever.

"Ooops, sorry, are we interrupting anything?"

Suddenly the room was filling up with people,

bright, happy partygoers in sparkling dresses and smart suits. James and Alice walked in with their parents, followed by Steve's father, Eric Lambert, and his guests. They all made a beeline for Jenna and Steve, who were now standing self-consciously apart and avoiding each other's gaze.

"Hello Jenna, nice to see you again." Eric Lambert shook her hand warmly. "Are you the one to ask when I need extra clues to solve the mystery?"

"You can ask, but I'm sworn to secrecy," Jenna answered, smiling and holding the gaze of his searching gray eyes. She liked this charismatic man but felt a little uneasy around him.

"What a superb bridle!" Alice noticed it at once. "You lucky thing. Look James, isn't it gorgeous?"

James had already seen it; he nodded silently and turned away to talk to his mother.

"You must be Jenna." A pretty, blonde girl, a few years older than Jenna, stood holding out her hand for Jenna to take. "Steve's told me all about you," she said pleasantly.

"Sorry, I should have introduced you." Steve suddenly found his voice again, and he seemed a little uneasy as he said, "Jenna, this is Rachel, er...our parents are old friends."

"There's a bit more to it than that," Rachel said, laughing. "We were childhood sweethearts, Jenna."

Jenna shook Rachel's hand and noticed, with an unwelcome stab of jealousy, her expensive-looking dress that accentuated her voluptuous figure.

"Hi, Rachel, it's nice to meet you. Look sorry, I'm supposed to be working, I'll see you later." Jenna excused herself and hurried thoughtfully back to the kitchen.

***

There was an air of expectancy pervading every part of the hotel on Christmas Eve. Jenna noticed it when she woke up and her happy mood stayed with her all day. After breakfast had been cleared away, Angie gave her daughter the rest of the day off and, as the sun was shining, Jenna decided to give Tufty a really thorough grooming and make a fuss over him. She felt a surge of guilt when she realized she couldn't remember the last time she'd done this, as now she had Gold to lavish her attentions on. Tufty wasn't too bothered. He liked being groomed when he was in the mood, but he got a little bored with having his mane plaited or his tail washed, and thought it all rather silly and unnecessary at his age. Today he felt restless and fidgeted at the end of his lead rope, the other end of which Jenna had tied to the railings that encompassed the yard.

"Keep still, Tuff, I've nearly got the tangles out, then you'll be beautiful again," Jenna soothed as she pulled at his knotted tail with a plastic curry comb.

Tufty couldn't care less about being beautiful. He wanted to go and roll in the muddy end of the paddock and then have a trot around the field as fast as his poor old legs could carry him. He felt tired but he also felt unsettled, and he wished Jenna would leave him alone and go and fuss over Gold instead.

"You're not nearly fat enough, despite all that food you've been getting, I wonder if you need a visit from the horse dentist?" Jenna looked in his mouth but saw nothing but a sturdy set of long, yellow teeth. Anxiously she ran her hand over his back and ribs and there was a sting in her heart as her fingers explored the jutting bones. She'd noticed this a while ago and had been giving him dippers of Gold's pasture mix for a couple of weeks now but there was no visible improvement. Gold had to have specially balanced food that would give him the energy to do his work without sending his high-strung thoroughbred brain into orbit.

She brought Tufty another bucket with a sizeable feed and watched to see how he ate it, but it went down easily with nothing to suggest that his teeth were giving him problems. Perhaps Mr. Penrose might have some ideas about feeding him, she thought to herself. I'll walk Tufty down there and see if he's in.

She untied his headcollar rope and led him down the drive to the row of cottages on the edge of the village where Mr. Penrose lived. Tufty pulled at the rope and jogged stiffly, which made Jenna laugh as he tossed his grizzled head and pretended to be a wild young stallion. She'd never known him so lively. Mr. Penrose was in his garden, apparently tidying an already spotlessly tidy greenhouse. He heard Tufty's hoof beats and came out to see.

"Hello, young Jenna, come to wish me a merry Christmas have you?" He smiled, revealing a perfectly white set of plastic teeth.

Jenna explained why she had come and then watched in silence as Mr. Penrose ran his hand over Tufty's flank before standing back and staring at him for a very long time.

"I think what's wrong with him, is the very same thing that's wrong with me," the old man said slowly.

"What's that?" Jenna asked.

"Chronic old age! It gets us all in the end, if we're lucky."

"Is that all? Does that mean I don't have to be too worried about him?" Jenna asked.

"No, I'd be more worried about acting in that play your mum and dad are putting on for Christmas – you want your head examined if you're serious about galloping about in the dark. You could kill yourself."

"Michael, the director, says it will make it more authentic having *real* horses." Jenna didn't like to admit the idea had been hers.

"You'll end up in a *real* hospital if you're not careful. I had that director fellow around here a while back wanting to know what I knew about the Goldsmith twins. I don't know how old he thinks I am, but that was at least a hundred years before my time!"

"Dad told him to ask you, as you know so much about the local history."

"I know that some things are best left alone. It

41

doesn't do any good to make fun of tragic events like that. It was terrible what happened with those brothers, and dragging it all up again is a sad mistake; I'm telling you, no good will come of meddling with the past, and troubled souls like that ought to be left to rest in peace." Mr. Penrose seemed quite upset.

"Michael's only based it very loosely on the twins' story, most of it is made up. Anyway, you said yourself, it was years and years ago."

"Bad things hang around a long time in a village like this; there were things that happened then that were still being whispered about when I was a boy," he said, pushing his false teeth forward in a most disconcerting way.

"What kind of things?" Jenna wished that Mr. Penrose would just come out and tell her instead of hinting mysteriously and expecting her to guess.

"Suspicions about what really happened between the Goldsmith twins mostly, and accusations about inheritances too. There were families in the village back then who thought they had more right to be living at the Green Horse than those who were."

"Who thought that?" Jenna asked.

"Relations of the Goldsmith twins, that's who. Instead of the relations of those who might have profited from a very convenient murder. As I said before, a nasty business and best left alone."

Jenna decided she wasn't in the mood for village gossip, especially gossip as old and cold as this. She deliberately changed the subject. "Mum tells me that your daughter is working for us over Christmas."

"That's right, so she'll let me know what's going on," the old man chuckled and turned to go back to his greenhouse.

Calling good-bye, Jenna led Tufty home.

"I don't suppose there can be much wrong with you if you can still dance like this." She smacked his rump affectionately as he passed through the gate and he made a passable attempt at a buck in reply.

***

To her surprise, when Jenna got back to the yard it was full of people; guests and actors, that was obvious by their odd costumes which were a stab at the 19th century with not much attention to detail. Jenna smiled as she noticed a lot of wristwatches and cell phones among the frock coats and full-skirted dresses.

It was the first organized "act" of the event and something significant was going on. The guests strained to listen as the two actors playing Abram and Arnold, the feuding brothers, had a loud and very staged argument. Jenna pushed forward to catch what was going on and then realized with a start that this was the last thing she'd have done if the row had been for real. There was something very liberating about standing and enjoying the action, instead of turning away, which her natural reserve would normally have had her do.

"What are you doing later?" James had sidled over to her. He looked very dashing in his frock coat, dark trousers and bright waistcoat, a costume especially hired for the weekend.

"Riding out. If Steve lets me borrow Spiral, do you want to come along on Gold?" Jenna looked at James as if for the first time. She had forgotten how handsome he was, especially in his costume, which really suited him.

"I'd love to." His smile told her that he really meant it.

"What's happening here?" she asked.

"I don't think those two are getting on too well," James replied with some irony as Abram pushed Arnold into a pile of conveniently placed straw bales.

"You don't say!"

They watched, fascinated, as the brothers wrestled and tumbled across the yard, shouting 19th century abuse and accusing each other of all sorts of dreadful things.

"Shouldn't you be taking notes?" Jenna asked, "I hear there is quite a good prize for the person who solves the murder."

"It's all going in up here." James tapped the side of his head and winked at Jenna, "and I don't trust that Abram chap as far as I could throw him; his eyes are too close together and I noticed at breakfast that he puts salt on his oatmeal!"

"Oh dear, that's it then, hang him!" Jenna

laughed, as she turned away to find Steve to ask if she could ride Spiral.

Jenna shivered slightly as she crept down to the stables in the dark to ride for the second time that day. The contrast between then and now could hardly have been greater. Then the sun had been shining, offering welcome, wintry warmth to her and James as they'd hacked out happily through the lanes. They'd only walked and talked, but she'd enjoyed the company, liked riding Spiral, who was tall and placid, and loved seeing Gold with James on top. Then she'd worn her old, familiar riding clothes, half-chaps and sneakers. Now she wore mahogany-topped leather boots and a large, dark coat of her father's that completely covered up the costume she was dressed in, which turned her from a 15-year-old girl of the 21st century into a grown man from the 19th. She had been careful not to be seen by any of the guests, some of whom were taking their roles of amateur sleuths far too seriously, asking questions and poking their noses into all sorts of things around the hotel. One lady, Mrs. Fry, had even been found listening at the kitchen door while her parents had been having their morning coffee. Dave had to politely, but firmly, explain to her that the plot was only being carried out in certain parts of the hotel, and that the kitchen certainly wasn't one of them. Jenna felt alive and exhilarated, despite having had a busy day with hardly any time to herself. An hour before, Michael had slipped her the parcel that contained her costume: light-colored breeches, a dark green, high-buttoned tail coat, boots, and a silk hat cover that she'd stretched over her skull cap – the only concession to the 21st century, and one her parents had insisted on. Jenna's hair was pushed into the hat, and she'd rubbed some black grease paint over her chin and jaw, which in the half-light looked a little like a five o'clock shadow.

A light was showing dimly from the stables; Steve, elegantly dressed in a costume similar to Jenna's, had arrived before her. He grinned when he saw her with her face blackened and in unfamiliar clothes.

"Don't forget to shave before you start waitressing later," he advised her.

"I won't," she smiled at him. "Anyway, I have the rest of the evening off after this; Mum's got Mr. Penrose's daughter working for her and says she can manage without me."

"I bet she thought she'd better get coverage for you, just in case you ended up a casualty," Steve told her, thinking he probably wasn't far from the truth.

Jenna brushed Gold before putting on his tack. She'd decided to borrow one of Steve's racing saddles to make it more authentic, but she dropped the stirrups down several holes because she wasn't used to riding quite as short as Steve. If Gold wondered what Jenna was doing, getting him ready for a ride in the dark, he didn't show it. His long chestnut ears remained pricked and he continued to pull at his hay until she slipped the loose-ringed bit between his teeth, making eating too difficult to be bothered with.

Jenna buckled the throat lash rather clumsily, her fingers feeling like thumbs, adrenaline coursing through her body as she thought about the ride ahead of her. She thought of Mr. Penrose and how he'd warned her not to get involved in acting out past tragedies and, although she didn't share his wariness, a delightful thrill of fear ran through her body. The low light, the cool night air, the smells of clean straw and warm horse all added to her excitement. Steve let himself into Gold's box and checked the gelding's girth, tightening it a hole and smoothing out the wrinkles with an experienced hand. Gently, he smoothed the chestnut's forelock and rubbed behind his ears, talking nonsense in soothing tones. Gold would never have made a successful racehorse, Steve had had to come to terms with that and he was glad Jenna had been able to buy him, but there was something glorious about the way the horse looked and moved that meant he would always be one of Steve's favorites.

"What's the time, Jen?"

"Half-past eight, they should be here soon. I hope so, I'm getting nervous, and I just want to get going now."

Jenna tried to imagine the scene inside the hotel. She guessed her mother would be just about serving the soup by now and that was the cue for the feuding brothers, Arnold and Abram, to start their fight. She hoped they wouldn't knock any furniture over and imagined her mother's anxiety if they got too near to the serving table where the splendid buffet was waiting. The fight would be broken up by a young actress playing the part of Kate who, in the plot, was dallying with the emotions of both brothers. Then the challenge of the moonlit ride would begin and Arnold and Abram would leave for the stables where Jenna and Steve would take over as their doubles for the actual ride.

"Shhh!" Steve suddenly put his fingers to his lips. "I think I can hear someone."

Jenna kept still and listened. The unmistakable sound of soft, running footsteps came from the yard, but then stopped. Jenna was sure she could hear breathing and it seemed to be coming from just outside the big stable doors, which stood open. Minutes passed and she exchanged a questioning look and mouthed the word "guest" to Steve who shrugged in response. Then they both heard voices, big, shouting voices, theatrically aggressive and getting louder. Whoever the third person was also heard the voices, and with a little gasp ran away towards the lower end of the yard, where there was a gate out into a paddock.

"It was probably that Mrs. Fry I was telling you about, she's taking the whole thing far too seriously," said Jenna as she and Steve walked out into the yard.

"Well, she's going to get scratched to pieces if she tries to get out on to the road through that field," Steve observed. "The hedge is full of bramble and blackthorn."

"Now we shall settle this once and for all!" Stuart and Paul came crashing into the yard, larger than life, pushing each other and laughing. "You can ride the donkey."

"Keep in character at all times, that's what Michael wants." Paul winked at Jenna.

"Fetch me my horse, boy," Stuart ordered Steve, who glowered back at him.

"Don't push your luck mate," he growled.

"Only joking, darling! Now, we'll wait here and have a little drink of this." He fished a hip flask from his jacket pocket, "while you two go and risk your necks in the name of art....or is it money?"

"Shut up, Stu," said Paul, "and you'd better not drink too much of that or Michael won't be giving you any money."

"Oh, leave me alone, don't forget I'm going to get murdered in an hour's time, I may as well have one more drink!"

Steve legged Jenna up into Gold's saddle, then led Gizelle from her stable and mounted her from the ancient block in the yard. He looked dashing, handsome and from another time, sitting tall in a wellcut coat on his wellbred horse. Jenna's heart melted when she looked at him. He could be a movie star, she thought. Gold sensed the excitement in the night air and began doing little half rears on the spot, bringing Jenna's attention back to the job at hand.

"Follow me, and try not to let Gold get too close to Gizelle's backside. I don't want you getting kicked." Steve spoke in a low whisper as they left the yard.

Jenna found it hard to keep Gold from jogging and harder still to avoid barging into the back of Gizelle, who humped her back and pulled terrible faces at Gold.

"Can I go in front?" Jenna gasped as Gold plunged his head down and tore the reins from her fingers, and she found herself wondering what ever had made her agree to this crazy night time stunt.

In front, Gold found he wasn't quite such a big brave horse as he'd thought he was. He saw ghosts behind every bush and tigers lurked in the shadows ready to bite off his tail. The path to the garden had never seemed so long to Jenna as she urged him forward, talking softly.

"We should have rehearsed this," Steve giggled from behind, "Gizelle thinks we're mad to be riding at this time of night."

"I agree with her," said Jenna from between gritted teeth. "You don't feel like swapping horses do you? Gold feels as though he's about to explode any minute!"

At that moment a crashing sound came from a hedge and both horses swung round in a blind panic. It was just a matter of luck that Jenna found herself still on Gold as Steve managed to swerve in front of her and bring both horses to a standstill.

"Are you ready?" Michael's disembodied voice called from behind the privet hedge.

Both horses snorted deeply and were ready to bolt again, but this time Jenna and Steve were ready for them.

"Can you come out slowly?" Jenna called to Michael.

"Sorry, did I startle them?" Michael asked.

"You nearly killed us both," said Steve without humor in his voice. "These aren't beach donkeys you know, they're thoroughbred race horses."

"You're both looking absolutely gorgeous, it's going to be so exciting for the guests. Are you ready for take off? I want you to gallop across the lawn then come round the back of the hotel and go across for a second time. Oh, and if you can shout a bit as you go, that would be very nice." Michael smiled at them.

"I will probably be screaming," said Jenna, "is that any good?"

Steve laughed, "What would you like us to shout?"

"Oh I don't know, things like 'get out of my way, you blackguard' or 'I'm going to beat you,' stuff like that," said Michael, unaware that Steve and Jenna were trying hard not to laugh at him.

"We'll do our best," they promised.

"Good. When I get the signal from Dave you can

set off, ah, here it is." Michael's cell phone rang three times then stopped.

"OK, lets go for it." Steve leaned over and squeezed Jenna's hand. "Try and keep behind me but if you get into trouble, just shout for me to stop and I'll try to."

Jenna nodded weakly, Gold started rearing again, catching her mood and her nervousness.

Michael was impressed, "I wish the guests could see him doing that," he said brightly, "now off you go, they're waiting for you."

Gizelle and Gold surged forward in one lurching movement and Jenna was almost left sitting in the bushes. She grabbed Gold's mane and pulled herself back into the saddle as they turned the corner and the large expanse of lawn lay lit up in front of them. She was aware of their hooves biting into the damp grass, kicking lumps of mud behind them as they galloped across. There was no chance of a controlled canter, both the horses had their blood up and they wanted to go. Jenna stifled a scream as the pace quickened, and they headed for the stretch below the patio. Out of the corner of her eye she could see a crowd of people and, despite the rush of wind in her ears, she thought she could hear the gasps of surprise as they thundered past. Now she was enjoying herself, her own pulse racing. She felt fearless and daring. Her blood was up and she was invincible, nothing could harm her, she felt charmed and was as happy as she'd ever been in her whole life. With great difficulty they pulled up beyond the shrubbery; Gold sprang and bounded on the spot and Jenna just grinned as she sat balanced and easy on his back.

"That was amazing," she gushed, "let's go again."

Steve gazed at her in the moonlight, her face was glowing with life and energy and exhilaration. He knew how she felt. It was why he rode races and risked his life on an almost daily basis schooling highly bred, unpredictable horses. He was anxious for her though; Gold seemed much more excited than he expected him to be.

"Are you sure you can hold him? He's pretty un-hinged by it all."

"We'll be fine, come on!" Jenna felt wild and un-conquerable and she set off at a long striding trot, clattering over ancient cobbles and through an arch-way, ducking her head as she went. This time, as they set off across the lawn, Gold knew what he was doing and where he was going. His gallop became even wilder and Jenna could hear nothing but the hollow pounding and drumming of their eight hooves on the ground. She tried to slow him at the shrubbery, but he didn't pay attention. She leaned back and pulled with all her might but still he didn't slow down. Suddenly her bravado left her and the cold grip of fear returned as she realized they were heading for the slippery lane that led to the yard. Gizelle's hoof beats were no longer with them and they made their terrible hurtling journey alone, each second taking them closer to an inevitable accident on the hard, unyielding ground. Think Jenna, she screamed at herself. Putting all her weight into her right stirrup and leaning hard on the right rein, she managed to turn Gold straight into the thick, evergreen laurel hedge that bordered the path. As they parted company, Jenna felt nothing but relief as she was flung from the saddle and into the prickly protection of the ancient bushes. Gold slithered to a halt, but managed to stay upright. Seconds later Steve was there grabbing his reins and calling anxiously to Jenna, who was picking herself, miraculously unharmed, from the hedge.

"I'm fine, there's nothing broken. Don't you dare tell Dad what happened, he'd have a fit if he knew I'd fallen off again. Quick, lets get back to the stables, the guests will be here soon." Jenna was talking quickly and breathing deeply, trying to stop the shocked feelings that were welling up inside her, threatening to make her burst into tears. She was grateful for the darkness when Steve, understanding exactly how she felt, just took her hand and led her back to the stable without another word.

Chapter four

They found Stuart and Paul sitting in the tack room still swigging from their hip flasks and laughing uncontrollably at the slightest thing. Jenna and Steve exchanged amused looks before settling their horses and giving them a small feed as a special treat after their efforts that night.

"What's the plan indoors?" Steve asked when they'd finished.

"They'll eat their main course, then they'll hear shots fired before pudding is served, and they'll all rush down here to find Stuart lying in a pool of tomato ketchup. That will give Mum just enough time to clear away the buffet and get the desserts ready. Everything's been planned to fit neatly around the catering arrangements."

"I hope the horses don't get upset by all the people and the noise. Perhaps I'd better get changed out of these clothes and come back in my casual clothes to keep an eye on them. We don't want Mrs. Fry looking for clues in Gizelle's box." Steve was frowning at the thought.

As they left, they passed Michael carrying a plastic container of red, gloopy, fake blood.

"You were brilliant!" He was breathless and flushed, despite the cool night air. "The guests were astonished when you galloped past. Very authentic, excellent, excellent," he muttered as he hurried on.

"I can't imagine Stuart being a very authentic corpse," said Jenna, "not if he keeps laughing like he was just now."

"Perhaps the idea is for him to keep drinking until he passes out. No, that wouldn't do either, he'd probably start snoring and that would be even sillier." Steve started giggling at the bizarre idea of a snoring corpse and Jenna joined in. By the time they got to the back door of the hotel they were laughing hysterically and having to hold each other up. For the second time that evening Jenna knew she was very, very happy.

Jenna never did find out what sort of a corpse Stuart made. When she got back to the hotel she was greeted by her dad with the news that she'd been invited to join James and Alice and their parents for the remainder of the meal.

"I said yes on your behalf, I didn't think you'd mind," Dave said, "but you'd better get out of those clothes before anyone sees you. "

"But what shall I wear? I'll look a little bit odd

in ordinary clothes when every one else is in costume."

"You could wear your serving maid outfit …"

Jenna scowled at him. She wasn't alone in her dislike of the costumes that Michael wanted all the staff to wear when serving Christmas dinner.

"Well, perhaps not! You'll just have to go as a ghost from the future."

"Are there such things?" Jenna asked, quite liking the idea.

"Oh, I don't know! Just hurry up and put a dress on." He scooted her away just in time as they heard muffled shots and the guests began to surge out of the dining room.

Up in her bedroom, Jenna pondered on the strangeness of life as she inspected her newest bruises in the tall mirror on her wardrobe door. There was a large blue patch spreading across her right shoulder and down her arm.

"Well that puts wearing short sleeves off for a while," Jenna sighed, as she looked through her small selection of smart clothes.

Dismissing her favorite blue velvet dress, she chose a simple gray silk skirt and a matching jacket that she wore over an emerald green top. She brushed her dark hair and sprayed a little glittery hairspray over it to make it shine, then pulled it back from her face with two plain, gold hair-clips. After her earlier attempts, she decided against make-up except for a sweep of mascara, part of Alice's present to her, which emphasized her clear, honest eyes. All it had taken was a quick wash and a change of clothes. Staring back from the mirror was now a pretty teenager from the 21st century, rather than an unshaven man from another age.

Jenna felt shy at first when she entered the dining room, full of chattering guests, but no one took much notice of her because everyone was talking about the "body" that had just been found in the stable. She was warmly welcomed by Mr. and Mrs. Edwards who had had an extra place laid for her next to James, but after politely asking how her day had gone, the conversation quickly returned to the much more interesting, if grisly, discovery of the murdered Arnold.

"He'd been shot through the head, there was blood everywhere. I felt quite ill. Then we heard footsteps and I'm sure I saw Abram running away down the drive." Alice looked white and shocked, and Jenna wondered if she wasn't taking the whole thing just a little too seriously. James was making a joke of it.

"I hope your mum's saved some tomato sauce for breakfast tomorrow? I can't eat bacon without it!" he told Jenna.

The puddings were delicious and Jenna ate two helpings of plum tart and a bowl of trifle, realizing that she hadn't had anything to eat since a piece of cheese and an apple at lunch time. The room was noisy with cutlery banging on plates, the excited chatter of 50 voices, and the faint strains of some choral music drowning in the background. Jenna spotted Steve at another table and felt an unasked for and quite unreasonable stab of jealousy when she saw he was sitting next to Rachel. They were deep in conversation, smiling, nodding and laughing, at times with their heads almost touching. Jenna stopped torturing herself and turned to talk to James, who was easily as good-looking as Steve. He just isn't Steve, that's the problem, she thought sadly to herself.

It got even worse when the tables were cleared away and the dancing began. Rachel and Steve made a captivating couple; both danced with confidence and a vivacity that was enviable. After a slow dance with James where she was sure he was going to try to kiss her, she made her excuses and went to bed with rather a heavy heart considering it was nearly Christmas Day.

***

The atmosphere in the hotel on Christmas Day was wonderful. Everyone seemed to be walking around wearing a huge grin and Dave had never known guests to be so mellow, laid back and uncomplaining. Even Mrs. Fry, who was fast becoming a candidate for the Fussiest Guest of the Year award, was happy and smiling, wafting round the hotel taking pictures of anyone she could persuade to pose for her.

Jenna opened her presents in her parents' bedroom. She'd truly meant to get up early and bring them breakfast in bed, but she'd made the fatal mistake of pressing the snooze button on her alarm clock and, before she knew it, they were both up and about and on their second coffee. The feeling of anticipation as Jenna surveyed the sizeable pile of presents in front of her was delicious, and she savored it for a while before choosing a small, boxy present to start with. On opening it, she found a pair of delicate gold earrings that she liked very much. Next came a turquoise sweater, then some expensive watercolors, a cell phone, and a book about show jumping. Soon the bed was piled high with bundles of ripped wrapping paper and scattered with shiny foil bows. Jenna decided she loved all her presents except for some purple slippers that she wasn't too sure about. Her favorite present of all was a small painting of Gold's head, done by a local artist from a photograph that Dave had taken back in the summer. She put this beside her bed where it would be the last thing she looked at before going to sleep each night.

She gave her parents their presents, which were of the sock, handkerchief, and bubble bath variety. She had spent ages trying to think of more exciting things to buy them, but it was difficult when funds were limited. Anyway, Angie and Dave looked very pleased. It must take years of practice to look pleased when someone gives you socks for

Christmas, thought Jenna to herself, wishing she could be more inventive.

The horses had a special Christmas breakfast of sliced apples and carrots mixed with their usual rations and Steve had hung tinsel over Gold's stable door, just out of reach so he wouldn't try to eat it. It glittered and sparkled incongruously, showing up the age old dust and grime around it. Jenna skipped out his box and wheeled the barrow, piled high with straw and droppings, to the muckheap behind the stable block. Tufty banged at his stable door as she passed, pawing the ground, first with one front hoof, then the other.

"All right, I'm coming," she called to him.

Abandoning the wheelbarrow, she led Tufty out to his paddock and he danced and skipped beside her like a 5 year old. Steve laughed when she struggled to hold the elderly pony as he pulled at his rope and twisted his gaunt old body in an attempt at a buck.

"Whatever it is you're feeding him, I'd like some," he told her. "You'd never believe he was over 30 the way he's been behaving recently. He could do with a bit more weight though."

"I'm just giving him the usual mix, quite a lot of it, but he doesn't seem to be getting any fatter." Jenna sighed; Tufty was a great worry to her.

They watched from the gate as he careered stiffly around the field before finally putting his head down to pick at the sparse winter grass.

"Did you and Rachel enjoy yourselves last

night?" Jenna asked, trying to sound casual and not too curious.

"Yes, thank you. How about you? I saw you dancing with your boyfriend." Steve looked sideways at her, smiling to himself.

"James is *not* my boyfriend," Jenna said firmly.

"No? Well, Rachel's *not* my girlfriend, just in case you're interested and didn't want to ask," Steve told her.

Jenna turned away, so that Steve couldn't see her face flushed red with embarrassment, but she was glowing inside with a wonderful cocktail of feelings that stayed with her for the rest of the day and made her want to sing.

***

Dave, Angie and Jenna worked very hard that day. Jenna thought back to past Christmases when they'd eaten themselves silly, gone for a short walk, then crashed out in front of the TV until bedtime.

"This is more fun," she reassured her mother when they stopped for morning coffee.

"Are you sure, darling? I feel so guilty for making you work so hard, but you know what it's like. This place has to pay for itself or we couldn't afford to stay here."

Jenna shivered at the thought of leaving the hotel, which in a very short space of time felt like more of a home than any other place she'd ever lived in.

"I don't care how hard I have to work, as long as

we never have to go back to London," she told her mother. "I'm never going to live in another city."

"Oh, you may change your mind. You'll want to go to college in a few years and who knows what kind of career you'll end up having."

"I'm going to be a show jumper, it's not just a dream, Mum, it's what I really want," said Jenna in a voice little more than a whisper.

Angie smiled at her only daughter; she didn't doubt Jenna had the courage and determination to succeed, but she hoped with all her heart that Jenna would have the luck she would need as well.

The drama unfolded nicely during the day and although Jenna only heard bits and pieces of it as she went about her work, there was an air of tension and amused excitement. The actors hired for the occasion were certainly giving good value. There were plenty of heated arguments, many huddles of would-be detectives interviewing suspects, and a generally lighthearted sense of fun about the place. The action moved from the dining room to the garden, accidentally passed through the kitchens, (which didn't please Angie who was having a crisis with her Christmas puddings), and ended up in the conservatory for a grand summing up of all the evidence gathered so far. Then there was a period when the action was suspended for a couple of hours to give everyone time to rest before Christmas dinner was served.

It was during this time that Jenna got to see Alice. They lounged in Jenna's room and talked about horses and boyfriends. Jenna wanted to know all about Pete, Alice's latest, but she felt less comfortable trying to discuss her feelings for James in case Alice thought she was being disloyal to him.

"Oh, I don't care, he never discusses things like that with me," said Alice. "I know he's really keen on you though. There's a girl from school who phones him up all the time – she's really pretty and nice, but James just isn't interested. I'm sure it's because he thinks he's in love with you. Don't you like him at all? I can't imagine how anyone could fancy him, but then I'm his sister and he probably thinks the same way about me!"

"I do sort of like him," Jenna admitted slowly. "I think he's really good looking and he's kind and thoughtful and all that. The trouble is I keep comparing him to Steve."

"I had a crush on Mr. Bennet, my math teacher last year. It was awful; I kept following him about like a lost puppy. It's sort of nice too, though, older men seem so much more sophisticated and intelligent." Alice had a faraway look as she remembered.

"What's Pete like?" Jenna changed the subject deliberately, rather cross that Alice had compared her feelings for Steve to a schoolgirl crush on a math teacher.

"He's tall, got a lovely smile, not conventionally good looking but nice all the same. He's 16 and is going to be a doctor. The worst thing about him is he doesn't like horses so I don't suppose it will last long," she said philosophically.

"Most boys don't like horses," said Jenna, "not in the way that we do, anyway. Not really love them, even the ones who can ride – it's definitely more of a girl thing."

Alice yawned and stretched out on the bed.

"I'm really enjoying this Christmas. It's great fun having something to do instead of watching TV all the time. It's really difficult though, trying to work out who did what and where – not to mention why! I bet you know who did it, how much would I have to give you for some extra clues?"

"Michael told me the whole plot, but it was so complicated I've forgotten most of it," Jenna laughed. "Anyway, I was sworn to secrecy, the honor of the hotel is at stake and the secret will die with me," she finished dramatically.

"What do you think of Abram? I hope he's not the murderer, I think he's really gorgeous. He was talking to me at lunch – I'm sure he thinks I'm at least 18."

"You looked it in that dress you were wearing, it's gorgeous, those costumes really suit your family. Perhaps you're a throwback from another era, here to haunt us all."

"You should see the one I'm wearing tonight. Mum went a bit mad when she knew we were coming here and it was to be period dress; she went to a theatrical outfitter in London and hired half their stock! I bet we don't get to wear it all."

Jenna looked at her watch.

"There's just about time for coffee before I have to go and help Mum again. Come down to the kitchen with me, and I'll see if there are any home-made biscuits left."

The girls ran down the stairs in their stockinged feet, jumping down two at a time and going so fast they almost bumped into Dave as they raced down the corridor to the kitchen.

"I was just coming to find you two. Your mum's panicking and she sent me out of 'her kitchen' to ask you where the book about napkin folding is. Oh, and could you get some sprigs of holly from the bush by the stables, she wants lots of berries if possible."

The phone rang in the reception area.

"I'd better answer that. Can I leave it with you?"

"Of course," said Jenna. "The book's on my bed-side cabinet, could you get it for me?" she asked Alice. "I'll put my boots on and go down to get the holly, then I'll meet you in the kitchen for coffee. I'll only be five minutes, put the kettle on while you're waiting."

Jenna's boots made a crunching noise on the grav-el path, and she stuck her hands deep in her pockets to keep them warm. The day had been sunny, but now the clouds were gathering and night was on its way. She worked quickly because of the cold, and she'd soon snipped off several berry-laden holly sprigs with her mum's clippers. She gathered her prickly harvest gingerly in her arms and set off back to the hotel.

As if from nowhere a dark, cloaked figure exploded on to the path, knocking Jenna sideways and spilling the holly on to the gravel.

"Hey, careful," Jenna shouted, more surprised than cross. "You can't get out down there," she added, rather unnecessarily as whoever it was would be well out of earshot. "Not unless you want to climb over a very high, prickly hedge anyway," she said, addressing herself now.

Picking up all the holly took a little time and the incident had, understandably, unnerved her. Then Jenna smiled to herself. Of course, it must be some part of the plot that she'd forgotten about. She hadn't recognized the actor, but then it had happened too quickly to see much and people looked so different in costume.

"I'll take the holly to mum, then I'll find dad and ask him," she said to herself, setting off towards the hotel at a jog.

Slipping out of her boots at the back door she padded into the kitchen and laid the holly down on one of the many shiny, steel work surfaces. One of the two kitchen helpers looked up from the vegetables she was preparing and smiled at Jenna. Angie, who was piping cream into pastry horns, waved a sticky hand at Jenna.

"Thanks darling," she called.

67

Jenna headed for the reception to find her dad, thinking how quiet the hotel was and imagining all the guests busy in their rooms, getting themselves ready for Christmas supper which was due to begin in half an hour. She jumped when she heard a stifled scream and Mrs. Fry's unmistakable voice saying, "Oh, it did give me a fright, I didn't think we were starting again until later. Now, where's my little notebook? You know, I thought it was a bit odd when I saw that girl in the..."

"Oh my god," she heard her father gasp.

Jenna turned the corner to see the frightening sight of Alice, crumpled in an awkward, unnatural position, at the foot of the elegant staircase. Her hair spilled out in a spiky blonde splash against the deep red of the carpet and Jenna was deeply shocked by the angle of Alice's left leg and by the deathly pale grayness of her usually glowing skin.

"Jenna, get your mum, I'll call the ambulance. Mrs. Fry, could you stay with her please?" Dave was gone within a second, and Jenna ran sobbing to the kitchen with Mrs. Fry's nervous giggle ringing in her ears.

"What do you mean, look after her? She's only acting... isn't she?"

A few minutes before the ambulance finally arrived Alice was conscious, but Mrs. Fry wasn't, having collapsed in a wobbly, jellylike heap when she realized that Alice really was injured and not part of the plot.

Angie and Jenna had put Mrs. Fry in the recovery position and there she lay, in the way of everything, covered with a tartan travel rug to keep her warm. Alice was in a great deal of pain from her very obviously broken leg. Her mum and dad were with her, soothing her and saying how brave she was being, but what did she expect if she would insist on running about in her slippery socks?

"I wasn't running," Alice protested, "I was walking, and I was pushed!"

"It's all right." Her father stroked her face. "It's the sort of thing that could happen to anyone."

"I was pushed," said Alice crossly, "from behind, I felt it."

"Who by?" Dave asked, stepping over Mrs. Fry.

"Don't think about it now, sweetheart." Her father shook his head at Dave and raised his eyes slightly to indicate he thought she was confused.

"Oh, at last, thank goodness," Angie said as an ambulance man breezed through the hotel entrance.

"Merry Christmas everyone!" he said cheerfully. "Have you got two victims for us? I was only told about one."

"Mrs. Fry has just fainted," Angie explained. "Alice is your real casualty."

"We'll check her over anyway. Jim," he called to his partner, "you can see to Mrs. Fry here, and I get to chat up the pretty one." He smiled at Alice who smiled back and visibly began to relax now she was in the safe, experienced hands of the paramedics.

Jenna kept reminding herself of the expression "the show must go on," as she helped her mum and dad to make their first Christmas dinner at the Green Horse Hotel a success. There were a few awkward moments when guests asked what had happened to the Edwards, who had all gone to the local hospital with Alice, and Jenna got quite tired of explaining about the accident. Mrs. Fry recovered remarkably quickly after she'd regained consciousness and found herself looking up into the rather handsome face of Jim, the young paramedic. She'd requested a large brandy and had been the life of the party ever since.

Abram, the chief suspect in the "murder investigation," made a brief and very dramatic entrance just before the puddings were brought out. The lights in the room had been dimmed to enhance the effect of the flaming puddings, making his appearance all the more startling, and one lady guest screamed. He was an eerie sight, and Jenna felt the hairs on the back of her neck stand up as Abram staggered into the dining room, disheveled, wild-eyed and protesting his innocence between anguished sobs for his dead brother. Some of the guests, getting rather carried away by the realism of the acting, started to call out, accusing him of killing Arnold.

"Those are just crocodile tears," called out Mrs. Fry, brave now after the brandy, "we all know you wanted him dead!"

"Yeah, that's right, you shot him, mate," shouted a

man in a loud, yellow, checked waistcoat which Jenna thought looked more like dodgy horse dealer than 19th century chic.

"Doesn't anyone believe I am innocent?" Paul was seriously over-acting by now, but the guests loved it.

"No!" they all shouted together.

"Then I shall go and you must not grieve for me."

He ran from the room, which erupted with chattering voices, and Dave had to bang the dinner gong three times before he could steer his guests' attention back to the food and the less dramatic, but still rather touching entrance of the Christmas puddings, alight with fluid blue flames licking the sides of the rich, black, currant-filled domes. Mr. Lambert raised his glass and proposed a toast to everyone at the Green Horse Hotel, and the guests rose to their feet as Angie passed by them carrying a flaming dish. She looked delighted with the effect, and Jenna found herself wiping away a tear of emotion when she realized what a huge thing they had achieved that day to give so many people such a special Christmas. Suddenly Steve was by her side.

"You look a bit pensive, is everything all right? I'm sorry to hear about Alice, but I'm sure she'll be better soon." He was like a kind big brother, she thought, grateful for his attentions.

"I was just thinking how happy everyone looks," Jenna told him, "Mum and Dad have worked so hard for all of this, and I'm so glad it's turned out well, despite Alice's fall. Has everyone in your party had a nice day?"

"Yes, thanks to you and Angie and Dave. Dad's delighted, everyone is really happy, especially Rachel. She's had some family problems recently. Her sister Kerry had a nervous breakdown and Rachel's been really worried about her. This has been a welcome break from all that."

"Poor Kerry, is she all right now?" Jenna asked, not really sure what a nervous breakdown was.

"A bit better I think, but she's been ill for as long I can remember, even when she was quite young she was in and out of hospital all the time. Anyway, what about you, have you had a happy Christmas?" Steve asked her, searching her eyes for the truth.

"Yes, different from normal and hard work, but, I've enjoyed it." She met his gaze and thought how lovely his eyes were.

"Is James at the hospital?" Steve asked.

"Yes, they're all there with Alice."

"Well, perhaps with James out of the way I might get to dance with you later. I wanted to last night, but you disappeared before I could ask you."

Jenna smiled her acceptance. A dance with Steve on Christmas Day would be the best present of all!

Everyone let their hair down that evening and the credibility of the murder mystery plot was suspended for a couple of hours while Michael acted as DJ and presided over the choice of music, which was definitely not 19th century. The dancing became fast and wild and even Dave and Angie joined in for a while, laughing and giggling like teenagers. It was a mild, still night and Dave opened the big glass doors on to the patio as people spilled outside to cool off and comment on the beauty of the stars twinkling overhead. Mr. Lambert started a conga, a long processional dance where all the participants are led along, in this case in and out of the shrubbery and up and down the many garden paths around the hotel. Jenna watched, perched on a stone seat, hugging her knees to keep warm. No one had noticed her there and she was too shy to join in, so she sat and smiled to herself, thinking how silly and childish adults could be sometimes. A faint rustle from the shrubbery behind her caught her attention and she turned her head in time to clearly see the pale face of a young woman peering through the evergreen leaves at the dancing snake of people. She was only there for a fleeting moment and, when she saw Jenna, she disappeared back into the darkness of the shrubbery and silently slipped away. Jenna's heart seemed to miss a beat, she stared into the blackness, wondering if she'd really seen what she thought she'd seen. Then she remembered the running figure who'd made her drop the holly. With all the fuss over Alice she'd completely forgotten to tell anyone about that. A mighty shiver ran through her body, and she leaped from the cold stone seat and ran to the comfort of the brightly lit hotel.

Chapter five

Jenna woke up on Boxing Day with a strange apprehensive feeling hanging over her, but she couldn't think why at first. Then she remembered the girl in the shrubbery and the conversation she'd had with her dad the night before. It had been very late, he'd been very tired and was rather inclined to think that Jenna had imagined everything.

"Are you sure it really was a face in the bushes? The light can play some funny tricks you know," he'd said as he collected glasses from around the lounge.

"Possibly, but it wasn't the light that knocked me over," said Jenna not unreasonably.

"No," Dave had to agree, "but you said they were in costume, so it must have been one of the guests getting a bit carried away with their role playing."

"You'd think they'd have stopped to apologize if it was one of the guests, and I definitely didn't know the girl in the shrubbery."

74

"Are you saying you think it was the same person?" Dave asked her, stifling a huge yawn.

"It could have been. Whoever knocked into me wasn't very tall; it might have been a girl or a woman, probably not a man."

"That reminds me, there was a phone call for you a few minutes ago, she didn't say who it was, just asked if you were there and I said you were and did she know what time it was, and she put the phone down. I probably sounded a bit cross, but it's well after midnight. I'm sorry if it was one of your friends but they really should call earlier."

This last bit of news had chilled Jenna and the feeling of unease was still with her the next morning. It was the third or fourth call she'd had, presumably from the same person. But whenever Jenna had tried to speak, the line went dead. It was beginning to spook her. Jenna tried to think of anyone at school she might have annoyed, or even one of her friends in London who she'd forgotten to send a card to. Try as she might, she couldn't think of anyone who'd want to pester her with these calls, and Jenna was getting scared, really scared.

Things didn't get much better when Jenna went down to the stables to do the mucking out. Strewn about the yard were flowers, dead flowers, white petals drooping, heads missing, leaves slimy, and rank from sitting too long in stale water. When Steve arrived, Jenna had fetched a broom and begun to sweep them frantically away. She could hardly bear to

75

look at them as they were scraped and smeared into a sad, small pile and shoveled into the wheelbarrow.

"What's all this?" Steve asked. He was bleary-eyed and thick-headed, and he wasn't looking forward to mucking out the stables.

"I found them all over the yard...someone's dumped them here in the night, it's really creepy." Jenna's voice wavered slightly.

"Lilies," said Steve, "probably stolen from the churchyard. What a horrible thing to do. Kids probably, though you'd think they have better things to do at Christmas."

"Steve," Jenna's throat felt tight and aching, "I'm really scared. I've had a few phone calls and a card...and now this. I'm sure someone's trying to frighten me...it's working too."

"What have the phone calls said?" Steve asked.

"Nothing, the line just goes dead. And the card wasn't actually nasty either, just odd and unsigned. And I suppose there's no law against sending someone flowers." Jenna tried to laugh.

"What makes you so sure the flowers were for you? I'm usually first here in the mornings," Steve said calmly.

Jenna thought about this for a while. Perhaps she was blowing things out of proportion. Then she had another thought.

"If Mr. Penrose gets to hear about this he'll say it's a ghostly apparition, probably Arnold Goldsmith, haunting us for making up stories about him."

"Anything's possible, perhaps we'd better keep quiet about it, we don't want all the guests down here 'ghost hunting' and disturbing the horses," Steve smiled. "Have you told your mum and dad about the calls?"

"They've been busy; if I'm still worried, I'll tell them after Christmas. But thanks, talking to you about it has helped," Jenna told him, she was beginning to feel a little foolish now. She wheeled the barrow to the muck heap and dumped the tattered white remains onto the steaming pile of muck.

Alice returned to the hotel after breakfast. Her cast made her leg stiff and useless, and she balanced precariously on her crutches, grinning from ear to ear.

"Do you like the color?" she asked Jenna, who was too shocked by how pale and tired Alice looked to notice the garishly colorful plaster. "I chose yellow and green stripes because those are my hockey team colors at school. Not that I shall be playing much hockey for a while."

Her parents looked tired too, having waited up most of the night for the leg to be seen by doctors, X-rayed, pronounced broken, and plastered. Apart from a bruise on her cheek where she'd fallen, Alice had been lucky to get away with just a broken leg.

"We've all had a horrible night," said Mrs. Edwards. "Not a wink of sleep, except for James, who curled up on the waiting room floor and snored away for ages!"

"I think we'll just go to bed for the rest of the day and see how we feel later," Mr. Edwards said, yawning loudly.

"I've prepared a room on the first floor for Alice," Angie told them, "I thought it would be better than stairs with that leg!"

She led them away, fussing and comforting them and offering to bring them a lovely cooked breakfast to their rooms.

The climax of Boxing Day was the resolving of the Murder Mystery, which was to take place after lunch in the lounge. It was to be Michael's big scene, where he got to play the clever detective who manages to unravel all the clues and solve the mystery once and for all. When Jenna got up he was strutting around the kitchen muttering to himself, occasionally stopping to make huge gestures with his hands, and when she spoke to him he was too engrossed to hear her. The weekend was set to end on a dramatic note with one last twist to the tale of murder and tragedy and Michael was going to play his part for all it was worth. Jenna had woken up tired and wasn't sure she had the energy required for the day in front of her. Finding the flowers had spooked her and, on top of that, she couldn't get the enigmatic face of the girl in the bushes out of her mind. After breakfast, she decided to take Gold for a ride and it wasn't until she was up on his back and riding down the quiet lanes that she felt her like herself again. It was a moist, dull day, but the air was warm for December and full of the winter smells of damp vegetation and household fires. She trotted past cozy cottages with windows that glowed with a warm, friendly light. Gold felt fresh and enthusiastic, his stride eating up the road and carrying her forward, faster than Steve would have allowed her to go, but he wasn't there to stop her. Gold pulled to be allowed to canter when his hooves touched the soft muddy surface of the track leading to the woods, and Jenna let him go, needing the thrill of his speed to re-energize herself. Soon the canter became a gallop and they streamed up the sloping track effortlessly. Jenna stood lightly in her stirrups and felt the wind drag tears from her eyes and across her face. With her vision compromised, she put her faith in her horse to find his way. Gold didn't want to pull up when the lane met the road, and he danced across the tarmac causing a slow moving car to swerve. The driver shouted something rude at Jenna, and she felt herself blushing from embarrassment as she got control of her excitable horse and trotted forward, along the road that would take them back to the hotel. As she passed the entrance to a farmer's field that Steve used for training his horses, she wondered if she dared take Gold in there by herself and try the jumps that Steve left up for practicing. Their golden rule was never to jump alone, just in case something happened, but Jenna was feeling reckless. She also worried as she realized the days were quickly passing and the Talent Spotters competition was only a week or two away.

"We'll just trot over a couple of little ones," she told Gold as she unlatched the gate.

Trotting around the edge of the big, flat field, she managed to get Gold under some sort of control by using her position to help her stay strong in the saddle, rather than clutching at the reins when he tried to take charge. Feeling confident, she trotted calmly into a brush fence that stood at less than three feet tall. Gold pricked his ears and whisked over the jump as if it wasn't there. Automatically looking for the next fence, they rode towards another brush, this one taller and wider than the first, but Gold made nothing of it. Jenna began to enjoy herself and, feeling braver than she had in quite a while, she cantered right around the field before setting him up for a substantial stone wall topped with a heavy pole. Gold leaped forward when he saw what she wanted him to jump and tore the reins from her hands in his enthusiasm. They met the wall fast, but perfectly, and Jenna's spirits soared and her heart almost burst with love for her spectacular horse. Seeing the next jump in the line, a big open ditch, which Jenna had never had the courage to tackle before, Gold assumed she wanted him to jump it. He increased his speed, his enthusiasm getting the best of him as he ignored his rider's polite request to steady his pace. Jenna said a word she wasn't allowed to use and shut her eyes as the ditch and rail rattled towards them.

She threw her body forward as he leaped and felt him stretch his back, waiting for the crash and the fall that was about to come. Landing softly he galloped on, and they'd covered half the field before Jenna was able to gather up her reins and stop him, skidding slightly on the greasy, wet grass. Gold was blowing and Jenna felt sweat trickle down her back. She hardly dared think about what they'd just done and when she turned her horse to walk slowly back to the gate she passed the ditch and was shocked to think she'd just jumped it, but mixed up with the shock was a deep well of delight and wonderment at her amazing horse who had made so little of it.

"If only I could control you in between the fences," she told him as they trotted home, "we'd be unbeatable!"

***

Jenna stood at the open door of the lounge, still in her riding clothes, and was in time to hear the collection of evidence during the past two days. Each guest took turns to solve the mystery, and the one nearest to the "truth", as judged by Michael the famous detective, would win a whole crate of champagne. Steve was speaking for his party when she got there, but his solution was so weird and convoluted, Jenna found it hard to follow. It wasn't until James got up to speak that she began to concentrate.

James was in costume, as was Alice, but the effect of hers was rather spoiled by the green and yellow plastered foot poking out from beneath her dress. He spoke well and with confidence, and Jenna could see he was enjoying being the center of attention.

James is on the wrong track, she thought to herself. She tried to remember the plot line that Michael had explained to her, but it seemed like such a long time ago.

"But what I don't understand," James admitted to his audience, "is who was the hooded figure in the stable yard on the night that Arnold was shot? I've kept quiet about it until now because I didn't think anyone else had noticed, but I'm completely confused as to who it was."

"What hooded figure?" asked Michael.

"I saw her too," said Mrs. Fry. "Twice! Once in the stables after the shooting and once on the landing outside my bedroom…it was a woman in a black cloak."

"Was it Kate?" asked Mr. Lambert.

"Was Kate in love with Abram, or was it Arnold?" Jenna whispered to her father as he joined at the doorway. She wished now that she'd paid more attention.

"Both, I think," he whispered back.

Everyone looked at Mrs. Fry who held her finger to her lips in a thoughtful way.

"No, she was shorter than Kate, I think," answered Mrs. Fry.

"Well, I can't imagine who that was," said Michael, genuinely puzzled, "though I do know that this hotel has a reputation for being haunted."

There were murmurs around the room, and several people said they too had caught glimpses of a cloaked figure.

Mrs. Fry got up to give her account, which was very convincing. It wasn't surprising, thought Jenna, considering how many hours the old lady had spent searching for extra clues.

Next it was Michael's turn, and he shook slightly with nervous excitement. He overplayed his part of detective wonderfully and he had the audience laughing one minute and acting shocked the next as he shouted accusations and crashed around the room in true melodramatic style. The finger of guilt seemed to be pointing towards Abram who had mysteriously disappeared after his brother had been shot, and Michael seemed to be taking his absence as proof. The remaining cast, those that hadn't been murdered or run away, sat looking suitably subdued and Jenna was impressed by their professionalism and wondered if their families had missed them at Christmas.

She looked idly out of the tall French windows that opened on to the garden. The afternoon was dull and the light fading fast, despite it not being late. The sight of a running figure across the lawn made Jenna gasp audibly and several people turned to look. To Jenna, at first glance, the girl might have been the one she'd seen the night before, hiding in the bushes, and it sent a shiver down her spine until she recognized her as the actress who played Kate. As Kate got nearer, Michael moved to the windows and opened them in time for her to stagger into the room where she made a loud and, Jenna thought, rather hammy confession. She told the gathering that it was for the love of Abram that she had agreed to shoot Arnold, but after she'd done it Abram refused to marry her as he'd promised, so she'd shot him too. Dramatically, she pulled a pistol from her cloak and told the world she was going to shoot herself, before running into the garden where the gun went off, leaving a stunned silence in the lounge.

Suddenly the room erupted with babbling voices and the tension broke. Soon there was laughter from people boasting about how they'd known it was Kate all along, and how they'd never trusted Abram and it served him right for treating Kate so badly.

"We have a winner, ladies and gentlemen!" Michael stood on a chair and bellowed across the room. "Would Mrs. Fry like to come and collect her prize?"

Everyone cheered as Dave presented some flowers and a crate of champagne to Mrs. Fry who was almost crying with delight.

Jenna shook her head and smiled to herself at the way everyone seemed totally wrapped up in the plot, almost as if they believed in it. Steve and Rachel came over to see her.

"What a performance!" Rachel smiled. "I never suspected her for a minute."

"Women are always more deadly than men," said Steve, smiling at Jenna.

"I've really enjoyed myself, Jenna, I haven't felt so relaxed in ages. You and your family have been brilliant hosts," Rachel said.

"I'm glad you've had a good time." Jenna just couldn't help liking Rachel, despite not wanting to because of how she felt about Steve.

"I've been trying for days to persuade Steve to take on one of my horses to train. He's a real star and winning everything with his current trainer," Rachel told Jenna, "and Steve's finally agreed to help me fetch him home and take him on for the next season."

"She wore me down." Steve seemed a bit uneasy.

"But that's good isn't it?" asked Jenna who was excited at the thought of a new horse on the yard. "I wouldn't have thought you would have needed much persuading. Where is he at the moment?"

"That's the trouble," Steve told her, "He's over in the States, so we'll have to fetch him right away if I'm going to race him this season. But the trip will take at least two weeks."

Jenna did a bit of mental calculation.

"But that means you'll be away for the Talent Spotters Competition!" Her disappointment was clearly written all over her face and to her alarm, tears began to prick behind her eyes.

"I know, and I'm really sorry Jen, but you'll be fine without me. I've already asked James if he could give you a bit of moral support…Jenna, come back."

Unable to hide her tears any longer, Jenna rushed from the room.

She found herself in Gold's box a few minutes later and was thankful that she hadn't met anyone on the way. By now she was feeling a bit silly that she'd reacted by crying. After all, she told herself, Steve didn't have to consider her whenever he did anything. He was a totally free agent and could go off to America whenever he liked, and take whomever he liked with him. She wished, though, he hadn't asked James to give her "moral support," whatever that meant. It sounded just like another phrase for baby-sitting, and Jenna squirmed at the thought of the two of them talking about her...perhaps it wasn't just the two of them – perhaps Rachel had been part of the discussion too.

"I'm just going to have to be more independent in future," she told Gold, who was licking her fingers, enjoying the saltiness of her damp hands. "Somehow or other you and I have just got to be ready for that competition…and we have to do well, just to show them!"

Jenna was a bit embarrassed when she met James in the corridor later that day, but she needn't have been because his mind was obviously somewhere else.

"Hey, Jenna, have a look at this," he said excitedly.

He handed her a scrapbook that was full of cuttings, notes and old documents, some of which she recognized.

"Michael lent it to me, it's all the research material he collected when he was writing the story for the murder mystery. There are old diaries and ledgers from the hotel, cuttings from newspapers, official court documents. It's fascinating, did you know that Arnold and Abram Goldsmith really existed? Their quarrel was about inheriting the hotel, it belonged to their un-married uncle who died without leaving a will, and there was another person who had some sort of claim to it, a distant cousin called Cressida Goldsmith – she was a rich widow and both of the brothers wanted to marry her."

Jenna thought she'd heard more than enough about the Goldsmith brothers to last a lifetime, she stifled a yawn but turned it into a pretended cough when James glared at her.

"According to this," he went on, "after the steeplechase, Abram was drinking heavily at the inn, boasting about his win and telling everyone that if he hadn't won he'd have killed Arnold and that he'd left his pistol hidden at the stables all ready and loaded. Later, when Arnold's body was discovered, Abram was arrested, even though he protested he was innocent. No one liked Abram, and even though several people were drinking with him when they thought they'd heard a shot fired, he was so unpopular that no one stuck up for him until after he'd disappeared. By then it was too late. When he was arrested he claimed that he could prove he hadn't shot his brother because his gun was hidden in the stables, but when they went to look, it wasn't where he said it would be. So he said it must have been stolen, but no one believed him. It says here that he escaped before his trial and was never heard of again."

"I wonder where he hid it," said Jenna.

"It must have been somewhere easy to get at if he was really intending to shoot Arnold if he lost the race. You don't want to be scrambling around looking for something in a situation like that."

"What happened to the hotel after all this went on? If both brothers were out of the way I wonder who inherited it?" Jenna was suddenly curious.

"I don't know, perhaps it was Cressida, but it doesn't say here. We could probably find out from the village records. Do you want to go and ask at the church? The vicar might know where things like that are kept?"

"Good idea, he's bound to know, and Michael said he was very helpful with the script," said Jenna. "You go and I'll catch you up. I want to make a phone call first."

Jenna went to the office behind reception and waited until her father was busy on the other phone before calling the number she'd copied down from the local equestrian directory that listed saddlers, riding centers, horse trainers, horse dealers, and everything any horsy person might ever need. This was the first step in Jenna's campaign to be more independent of Steve and, when a nice man answered the phone Jenna explained that she needed some help with her show-jumping and she wanted to hire a course of jumps to practice over. She'd chosen The Oaks Show Jumping Center, even though it was a few miles away, because the ad had specifically mentioned that it specialized in helping difficult horses. She wasn't sure if Gold really was difficult, she only knew that she found him difficult and that was enough. She gulped when she heard what a two-hour lesson was going to cost, but she had earned some money by working over the Christmas break, so she booked her first session for the end of the week. She felt very pleased with herself as she put the receiver down and neatly wrote the details on a pad by the phone. Now she just had to arrange transportation for herself and Gold, but she would do that later…she remembered seeing a business card in the tack room with the name of a horse transporter Steve sometimes used. She would find it and call them, but for now she'd better catch James up and rescue the poor vicar who was probably sick of being pestered by people from the hotel!

Feeling much more positive, Jenna jogged down to the village, only to find James was already walking back through the long, narrow churchyard.

"The church was locked and, when I called at the

vicarage, the vicar's wife said all the records are kept at the council offices in Tuxford." James told her.

"What a shame, that's miles away. It would have been interesting to know if Cressida ended up owning the Green Horse," said Jenna.

"It would, because I've been thinking, if Abram didn't kill Arnold then the next most likely person is whoever was going to profit from him being dead and that must have been the person who ended up inheriting the hotel."

"He might have committed suicide," said Jenna.

"I suppose he might, I hadn't thought of that! Especially if he stood to lose the hotel and the woman he loved in one fell swoop." James seemed disappointed.

"I don't suppose we'll ever really know," said Jenna, "even if we do find out who inherited the hotel, it doesn't automatically mean they were the murderer."

They walked slowly through the graveyard, stopping to read the inscriptions on the stones. It was odd to think of all the people whose bones lay in the ground around them.

"Let's see if Cressida is buried here," said Jenna, a peculiar feeling suddenly came over her when she realized that they were probably standing within earshot of the remains of the very people they were talking about.

It didn't take them long to find the grave of Arnold Goldsmith. A simple granite cross marked

90

his resting place, but time and weather had faded the leaden letters that marked out his last message to the world. They searched for another hour until, in a far corner of the churchyard, almost as far away from Arnold as it was possible to get, they found Cressida. Her memorial was a magnificent winged angel carved from a pinky white marble, but the earth had settled over the years, so the stone had cracked and the angel was falling. The dates told them that Cressida had lived for more than 50 years after the death and mysterious disappearance of Arnold and Abram.

"Cressida Lily Goldsmith Walton," Jenna read aloud, "'Heaven has another angel'...I wonder if that's true!"

"And look," said James, tracing his finger around the weatherworn words carved on her stone. "'Loving wife of Frederick Walton, inn keeper of this village'. So she did get the hotel after all, though I suppose Frederick Walton might have bought it before he married her...bit of a coincidence though."

They both gazed at the stone angel, and thought about the woman whose remains lay beneath it.

"Jen…?" An odd expression passed over James' face.

"What's the matter?"

"I've just had a thought…the hooded figure, the woman everyone thought they saw who wasn't in the cast…what if it was Cressida?"

Jenna's skin tingled with this strange possibility.

Since coming to live at the Green Horse Hotel she found it easy to believe in ghosts, and other spirits. Then she remembered the running figure she had collided with, there was no doubt that it had been flesh and blood.

"I suppose anything is possible," she said.

"It all fits," said James' enthusiastically, "it may even have been what Mr. Penrose expected when he said nothing good would come of messing about with the past."

"Maybe," said Jenna. She wanted to believe in the ghost of Cressida, after all ghosts might be frightening but they couldn't hurt you…or could they?

"James," she said quietly, "can ghosts make telephone calls?"

James laughed out loud.

"What *are* you talking about?" he asked.

"Oh, nothing," Jenna answered, suddenly shaking off her pensive mood. "Let's go, I'm bored standing here. Do you fancy going for a swim?"

James wasn't big on swimming. He didn't like getting wet and he certainly didn't like getting cold, especially not in December, but the thought of spending an hour with Jenna in a swimsuit was enough to make him do all sorts of things he wouldn't normally do.

"That's a great idea," he told her, "I just hope your dad has turned the heat on high."

Jenna went on ahead and didn't notice when James, turning to leave Cressida's grave, accidentally kicked over a small, glass flower vase, scattering the contents across the path. Quickly he scooped up the white lilies and placed them, best he could, waterless and drooping, back in the shadow of the huge stone angel.

Chapter six

A few days after Christmas James and Alice left with their parents for home. Alice hopped out to her parent's large, posh car and eased herself into the back seat.

"Would you like to come and stay with us at Easter?" she asked. "I should be free of this thing by then," she pointed to her plaster cast, "so we'd be able to ride together."

"I'd love to...and I'm really sorry about your leg, I can't help feeling responsible in some way."

"It wasn't your fault, I must have slipped like dad said. I couldn't really have been pushed, could I? It's odd though, but I suppose when you bump your head you imagine all sorts of things."

Jenna wasn't sure. She couldn't find a rational connection between the running figure, the face in the bushes, and Alice's fall, but in her heart she was sure they were all linked somehow.

James didn't say much to Jenna, he just kissed both her cheeks in a rather detached, formal way, aware that his sister and both his parents were watching him.

"I'll call you sometimes," he whispered to her, "when I get fed up with studying!"

"I'd like that, and I'll see you very soon, at the show."

"I'll be there, don't worry," he promised.

Jenna waved until the car went out of sight. She asked herself if she would miss them then quickly dismissed the thought as she knew the answer. Of course she would, but she would be too busy with Gold to dwell on it.

Steve said goodbye to Jenna later that day after a rather unsatisfactory schooling session in the paddock when she had been completely unable to stop Gold from dashing flat out into his fences. Steve got cross with her more than once and shouted to her to sit up and use her seat – not her hands – to control him.

Despite the wintry, early January day, Jenna was steaming inside her fleece, wet from the inside and rain- soaked from the outside too. Her face was red and she had a smear of mud across her nose, but to Steve she still looked cute, so he put his arm around her and gave her a quick kiss on her cheek.

"Take care of yourself, sweetheart. Don't forget I'm only going for a couple of weeks," he told her, surprised at his own feelings, as he saw her struggling to hide her tears.

"I'm not sad because I'm going to miss you," she told him almost angrily, "it's because I'm worried about jumping Gold without you there. You know him better than I do," she added rather lamely.

Steve had arranged for Gizelle and Spiral to stay at his dad's stables and, when he drove them away from the yard, Jenna's feelings flooded over and she went into Gold's stable to cry on his shoulder. Gold didn't mind. He was lonely and restless with his two girlfriends away, and he enjoyed Jenna's company, even if she was making a silly, sniveling noise. He looked at her and then put his head down low and snorted deeply, blowing shavings up into the air in a big cloud. Jenna laughed at him and felt better.

"We'll show them!" she told the chestnut affectionately as she began to brush his sleek coat with the body brush she kept behind his manger. "We'll win that competition and show everyone what a great show jumper you are."

Gold agreed, in principle, to everything Jenna said, and if he wasn't completely sure what a show-jumper did, then he was nice enough to try his best for Jenna, whatever it was she wanted him to do.

The next morning Jenna woke to the sound of rain lashing the thin glass of her bedroom windows. She didn't need to open the curtains, she could imagine the dark skies and buffeting winds, and a wave of sadness swept over her when she realized that this was the day Steve and Rachel would fly out to America together to collect Rachel's horse.

But when she remembered that it was also the day when she'd booked her first lesson at The Oaks Show Jumping Center, she cheered up a little. Jenna looked at her clock, it was almost 8 a.m. and the lorry was arriving in two hours. Plenty of time for a hearty breakfast, she thought to herself, wondering why being lovesick over Steve hadn't taken her appetite away like it was supposed to.

The hotel seemed empty by comparison to the busy Christmas they had just had. Now there were only a few guests staying and Angie could manage without Jenna's help, so she ate a large bowl of muesli at the kitchen table and wondered what she should wear for her lesson.

"Thankfully there's an indoor school," she told her father when he came in with the morning paper, "so we won't get too wet."

"When's that competition you're so worked up about?" he asked her, thinking he really ought to take more of an interest in his daughter's hobbies.

"Saturday." She saw an anxious look pass across her father's face. "Don't worry, I know you're busy on Saturdays. James said he'd meet me there and help out. He passed his driver's test last autumn, and he's allowed to drive his mum's car."

"That's kind of him," Dave said, feeling relieved, but also rather guilty.

"How are you getting there?"

"I'm going to book the same person who's taking me today, someone Steve uses. I got the number from a card in the tackroom, and the woman sounded nice when we spoke."

"Well, have a good day and don't fall off, you seem to have had more than your fair share of tumbles lately."

"I'll try not to," Jenna told him, realizing she'd been on the floor more times than her dad actually knew about.

"What time will you be coming home?" Her father asked as he folded up his paper.

"Oh, I don't know. It's at least an hour's drive – probably not until teatime. I'll call you if I'm going to be late," she reassured her father, making a mental note to take her cell phone; she just hoped the battery was charged.

Jenna spent ages grooming Gold that morning. She brushed his silky, clipped skin, pale and mouse brown where the golden hairs usually sat with just the ghosting of gleaming tips now his coat was beginning to grow back. Jenna didn't like having to clip Gold, but the fast, hot work she expected him to do during the winter months made this necessary, and Steve clipped him for her when he did his own horses. She had to admit he did look very smart when he was done, but she missed the rich golden color that gave him his name. She oiled his hooves and brushed his tail, which she had washed the evening before. It had gone soft and rather fluffy, so she stuck it down with a slick of baby oil that Steve kept in the tackroom. She was wearing her black jodhpurs, ankle boots, and the leather half chaps that zipped up over her calves and made her feel very professional. On top she had her favorite, padded jacket, which was smart, though not very waterproof, but Jenna decided she'd not have to spend too much time outside, so it wouldn't matter.

The lorry drew up into the yard through the gates that Jenna had left open. A young woman jumped out of the cab and let down the ramp at the rear of the lorry. She didn't speak, just gave Jenna a vague smile as she pulled back the padded partition and held it open. The rain made everything shiny and dark, and Jenna shivered slightly as she led Gold up the ramp. She tied him quite short to the ring and went back for his saddle and bridle and her bag, which she slung up into the living area behind the cab. The truck was small, but had every convenience a horse or rider could wish for. Jenna cast her eyes around the living area that had comfy seats, a TV, a microwave, and even a shower room; the horse area had hayracks and mangers and a non-slip rubber floor. Jenna wasn't sure where she was supposed to sit, but the woman wasn't very approachable and didn't seem to hear when she asked, so Jenna settled down in the cab beside the driver, the engine roared into life and they were off.

"It's The Oaks Show Jumping Center, do you

know the way?" Jenna asked shyly. "I've got directions if you don't."

The woman nodded, "I know it," she said quietly.

"How long will the trip take?" Jenna asked.

The woman just shrugged, and Jenna gave up on conversation and slipped into thinking about the lesson ahead of her. She was very excited. This felt like a real adventure going off by herself with Gold, to practice over a proper course of fences instead of the adequate but rather makeshift ones she was used to. The day was dismal, but it failed to dampen Jenna's growing enthusiasm as the truck passed fields and hedges and made its way steadily along the narrow country lanes. When they got to the Tuxford junction, Jenna expected the woman to turn right instead of left, but her sense of direction was never very good, so she didn't say anything. Instead, she shut her eyes and tried not to think about Steve and Rachel who were probably at that very moment boarding a plane to America. She wondered if they were holding hands, then pushed the thought out of her mind. Steve had told her that Rachel wasn't his girlfriend, that it was just a business arrangement, but Jenna had seen the ease between the two and it looked more than "business" to her. She sighed and opened her eyes, looking around her for familiar landmarks. Her watch told her that they had been driving for about 40 minutes now, so they should be nearly there, but she was rather surprised to see the moors up ahead of them.

"I didn't think The Oaks was near Castle Hills,"

she said to the woman, anxious now in case there had been some confusion. Perhaps there was another equestrian center with the same name. "It's The Oaks at Stanford. That is the one you're taking me to isn't it?"

The woman nodded, but kept her eyes fixed firmly on the road ahead. Jenna studied her, her anxiety rising as she was sure by now they were heading the wrong way. She wondered if she would have to pay for the lesson even if she didn't turn up for it. Now Jenna looked at the woman properly for the first time. She was in her early 20s and quite pretty in an understated sort of way. Her fair hair was cut short, and though she was slightly built, she looked tough and her mouth was set in a hard line as if she was thinking about something or someone she didn't like. Jenna thought she looked familiar and wondered if she'd ever seen her before; perhaps she'd been to the yard with her lorry on a job for Steve. As the lanes became smaller and the hills loomed in front of them, Jenna was sure they'd come the wrong way and she rummaged in her bag for her mobile phone. At least I can call the center and explain what's happened, she thought to herself. Perhaps they'll give us proper directions and won't mind if I'm late. She sighed as the display on her phone told her that there was no signal.

"Some networks don't work up here." The woman's voice made her jump as it was almost the first time she'd spoken.

The truck slowed and Jenna heard the indicators ticking as the lorry turned into a bumpy, unmade lane. Gold whinnied anxiously from the back as the lorry swayed a little, then came to a halt in the entrance to what appeared to be a disused quarry.

"We're lost, aren't we?" Jenna decided to try to be cheerful, despite the rising feeling of disappointment at her missed lesson. "Have you got a map?"

"Oh, Jenna, you really have no idea why we're here, do you?" the woman sighed and turned in her seat to look at her younger companion.

A shiver of fear went through Jenna's body as she tried to make sense of the woman's words.

"What do you mean?"

"What I mean is, I've brought you up here because I think it's time we had a little chat," the woman replied quite calmly.

"B...b...but who are you? Have we met before somewhere?" she stammered, sensing now that something was not right about the whole situation.

"Me? I'm Kerry, and if I look familiar it's because you know my twin sister, Rachel."

Relief flooded through Jenna, of course that was who Kerry had reminded her of, a less glamorous version of Rachel. She'd never have thought they were twins though, but it was good to know she was a friend; for a minute or two she'd been quite spooked by the situation.

"Rachel's really nice," Jenna told her with a

smile, "she's been staying at the hotel.... but I suppose you know that."

Kerry's look was far from friendly, and Jenna's words dried on her lips.

"I've brought you here to tell you to keep away from Steve." Kerry stared straight ahead through the rain streaked windscreen.

"What?" Jenna exclaimed.

"You know what I mean, stop hanging around him, flirting with him, flashing your eyelashes at him, and pretending to be helpless so that he does things for you."

To Jenna, this outburst was almost funny, it seemed ludicrous.

"You've brought me and my horse all the way out here to tell me that?" she asked, angry and unable to believe what Kerry had done. "To warn me off because you like him yourself?"

"Me and Steve? Don't be so stupid, Steve belongs to Rachel!" Kerry's voice sounded low and dangerous, as if she was on the very edge of losing her control. "They've been engaged for ages, and they would have been married last summer if you hadn't come along."

"But I hardly knew Steve last summer," Jenna protested. "He told me he had been going out with someone called Louise, but that was over and he never even mentioned Rachel before I met her at Christmas."

"You're making that up, you've got a crush on

him…go on, admit it," Kerry hissed in Jenna's face. What about that bridle?" she pointed vaguely to where it hung behind them, "that wasn't supposed to be for you. I know it wasn't, I met Steve in the shop when he was buying it. It cost nearly two hundred pounds...it must have been for Rachel, he wouldn't spend that sort of money on a kid like you."

Jenna was genuinely shocked, she'd realized it was a lovely bridle, but not quite how lovely.

"OK, I admit, I do like him, but he doesn't feel the same way about me, I'm just like a kid sister to him", unfortunately, Jenna added under her breath.

"You would say that, but you don't know what this has done to my sister. She made herself ill over Steve when they split up, she was in hospital because she wouldn't eat anything, and I'm not going to stand by and let you ruin everything for her again."

"But Rachel seems fine," Jenna protested, sure that Kerry had got her wires crossed somewhere; "she and Steve are flying out to the States together today."

"No thanks to you, I know you tried to stop Steve from going, Rachel told me how you cried when they told you. You're just using emotional blackmail to make him feel guilty."

For a few seconds Jenna wondered if this was true. She hadn't wanted Steve to go, that was for sure, but she really hadn't meant to make him feel guilty; after all, she'd always known that Gold and his training were ultimately her own responsibility.

Kerry was muttering something under her breath now, and Jenna could only catch a few words, but they were not exactly nice words and, for the first time, Jenna began to be really scared.

"You will do as I say... " Kerry stared straight at Jenna, glaring into her eyes so hard Jenna could almost feel it. Suddenly, Kerry lunged towards Jenna and grabbed her by the collar of her jacket. Struggling to get free, Jenna opened the truck door and half jumped, half fell on to the hard, gravel track. Kerry landed on top of her, shouting abusive remarks and, for a few seconds, the two girls wrestled and twisted, rolling against the wheels of the truck. Jenna was a fighter and physically the two were quite well matched, but the older girl was completely enraged and had strength she wouldn't normally have had. Jenna's head struck a stone and blood trickled from the wound and seemed to excite Kerry further and her curses turned to a weird, angry laughter. Together they rolled against a granite gatepost. Jenna was squashed now and couldn't fight back, all she could do was lie motionless and cover her face as Kerry screamed and rained frenzied blows to her body. For a second her stillness seemed to affect Kerry, who stopped her attack just long enough for Jenna to get up on her feet and run away from Kerry, who did not try to follow. Jenna stumbled through a gateway and, unable to run any more, flopped down close to the hedge, not minding the brambles that seemed to reach out to protect her.

She gulped for air and tried to make her breathing quiet, as she strained her ears to hear sounds that would tell her that her assailant was near. The first thing Jenna noticed was the silence. The attack had not lasted long, but it had been so sudden and so unexpected and, despite her bruises, the worst thing about it had been Kerry's angry shrieking and cursing. Jenna didn't know how long she stayed pressed against the prickly, granite hedge, gaining strange comfort from its solidity and height. Slowly her heart rate became more normal and her head began to clear. She took deep breaths to try to center herself. She scanned the horizon for houses. There was nothing very close but Jenna could see a cottage, perhaps a mile away and best of all, from its chimney, a trickle of smoke rose gamely into the rain soaked sky. Not wanting to be seen, Jenna crept along the hedge that ran steeply up, vaguely in the right direction for the dwelling she was heading for. Not until she got to the shelter of a small belt of trees did she risk looking back. She could see the top of the horsebox, still parked where it had been, but there was no sign of Kerry. She thought of Gold, helpless and wondering, tied up in the back…surely Kerry wasn't mad enough to hurt her horse to get back at her? She quickly pushed the thought out of her mind and ran the last half mile to the cottage. With great relief she banged on the front door. She waited in the bare, newly made garden, which seemed so formal compared to the wild countryside surrounding it. She could hear a dog barking, but no welcoming footsteps. No reassuring, motherly woman came to offer Jenna comfort and call the police. Perhaps there's someone at the back, and they can't hear me knocking, thought Jenna and she opened the side gate to see. The dog came from nowhere and for the second time that day Jenna was ambushed and taken by surprise. She was only aware of a blur of curly white fur torpedoing towards her and then a sharp pain in her ankle as the poodle struck his target and held on. Kicking furiously with her other foot, Jenna cried out with pain and the injustice of this further attack.

"Stupid bloody dog," she screamed at it, finally managing to aim a kick, which propelled the dog satisfyingly skywards for a few feet. It landed on its smug little white paws and shook its carefully groomed head, yapping insults at Jenna as she closed the gate and retreated to the safety of the front garden.

Jenna felt completely alone. Her phone was in the truck, and the only house for miles around was empty except for a psychopathic poodle. Her beloved horse was being held prisoner, and she was bruised and frightened and accused of a crime she hadn't committed. She started to cry, shaking and sobbing loudly so that even the dog stopped yapping to listen to her. Jenna sunk down against the gate and wept, warm tears mingling with cool rain until common sense hit her, and she knew she had to do something.

She knew she had to go back down the hill to try to reason with Kerry and get her to take her home.

It was as simple as that when she was at the top of the hill, but her pace slowed as she neared the belt of trees and the memory of Kerry's pounding fists came back to her. Did she really want to go back and face more of that? Was Kerry still there? Stalling for time, Jenna climbed almost to the top of a sycamore tree and peered out from the naked, wintry branches. Keeping close to the trunk and thankful for her dark clothes, Jenna could see the lorry. She watched as Kerry got out of the driver's seat. She was speaking on her cell phone as she walked along the lane. She appeared to be scanning the fields, looking for something…or someone.

"Me, I presume," Jenna said aloud, answering her own question; she was too far away for her voice to carry. "Not worried about me are you, Kerry?"

Kerry got back into the car, and Jenna heard the door slam.

"What am I supposed to do now?" Jenna spoke again, as the sound of her own voice was strangely comforting. "I'm too scared to confront her and too worried to leave Gold by himself. If she thinks nothing of beating me to a bloody pulp, then she might do anything to Gold, especially if she knows how much he means to me."

The lorry was parked at an angle with the front end facing away from Jenna; the groom's door into the horse area was clearly visible and it gave Jenna an idea. She climbed down from the tree and scanned the field, which lay between her and the quarry entrance where the lorry was parked. She could feel her heart pounding inside her chest as she neared the rear of the horsebox. Dodging the range of the rain streaked rear view mirrors, Jenna undid the ramp bolts as silently as possible. She could hear the strains of the radio coming from the cab and she imagined Kerry, warm and dry inside, and it made her cross. How dare she? Jenna was fueled by her anger. She mounted the steps and slowly opened the door into the horse area. Gold was very pleased to see her. He'd been bored just standing there, his meager ration of hay had long since gone and there was nothing interesting to look out at from the small, barred window. Jenna patted his warm neck and was heartened by his familiar smell and companionship. She untied his rope and, slipping it over his neck, tied the other end to the ring at the side of his head collar to act as short, thick reins. The music from the radio reassured Jenna, particularly as she could hear Kerry's voice singing along to the familiar tune.

"God, how cool is she?" Jenna whispered to Gold, as she unhooked his partition, effectively freeing him from everything except the ramp, which was still firmly in place. Jenna jumped aboard his back, ducking her head to avoid hitting the roof, and reached across to the button that would lower the electrically operated ramp and allow them their freedom. She hesitated before she pushed it. This was the only part of the plan she wasn't clear about. High up on Gold's back, even without a saddle and bridle, she had the upper hand, but Kerry would be there in a flash, and she would try to grab Gold and perhaps pull Jenna off him. She looked around her for a weapon, but there was nothing in the back except Gold's empty hay net. It wasn't much, but Jenna took it and practiced a swing, the heavy rope and the metal rings were weighty enough to be of some use. Then she pushed the button.

The noise of the electric ramp making its painfully slow way to the floor galvanized Kerry into action, as Jenna had known it would. At the rear of the lorry Kerry was powerless to stop the ramp's descent but she stood on guard, arms widespread, blocking the exit and the two girls stared at each other in silence. When the ramp was horizontal, Jenna urged Gold on to it. He was reluctant, and dithered, sure she must be mistaken.

'Wait for it to reach the ground', he implored her with his body.

'No, go now', her legs insisted as blind fear made her kick her horse forwards.

Sure he was right, sure it wasn't safe, Gold wanted to do what Jenna asked, but nothing was going to make him set foot on this dangerous, mobile drawbridge. Instead, he sat back on his hocks and launched himself forward, clearing the whole ramp but landing badly, knocking Kerry sideways as she

110

tried to grab him. Jenna stayed on, though she never knew how. She just clung to Gold's back with every muscle and every ounce of strength she had left and felt the lithe, pent up thoroughbred stretch into a gallop along the hard track, taking her to heaven knows where. Anywhere was good, as long as it was away from Kerry.

They galloped on and Gold left the track and headed across the open hillside, scattering bedraggled sheep in their wake. Jenna sat easily, but didn't try to slow his pace; she knew it would be useless. He was hard enough to control with a proper bridle and bit let alone a headcollar with a rope for reins. Gold was fit from a thorough program of winter riding, and she felt he could have run forever, but Jenna tired quickly, weak from her ordeal. Knowing she was close to falling, Jenna tried a feeble pull on the thick, sodden rope. Feeling the gentle pressure across his nose, Gold responded immediately and, to Jenna's immense relief and surprise, his gallop became a canter, which became a trot, then slowed to a walk. She lay across his neck for a few paces to ease the cramp in her legs. She was lost, she knew that. But everything seemed much simpler now it was just her and Gold. She would find a road, ride along it until she came to a village, and then phone her dad who would sort everything out for her. She was almost jubilant as she turned Gold easily with her legs and seat and headed down the hill. The rain was persistent and had reached the inside of her jacket now. Her clothes clung to her and cold was setting in, but the adrenaline was still racing round her body, keeping her senses alert and ready for flight.

Gold's hooves sounded hollow on the tarmac when they eventually found a road. Jenna pushed him into a trot to warm them both, and she was delighted when he softened his jaw and neck and accepted the headcollar's contact on his nose far more readily than he'd ever accepted a bit. Stretching her aching legs downwards and sitting tall, she drove him forward into her hands and achieved one of the best, most controlled trots she had ever known. She slowed him easily when they came to a signpost, and Jenna knew her ordeal would soon be over when she read that the village of West Hatch was just one mile further down the road. She hoped there would be a shop; she was beginning to feel very hungry and she was shocked when she finally looked at her watch and realized how late it was. Mum will just be clearing up after lunch, she thought, longing for the hotel's warmth and brightness.

The lane was narrow and when Jenna heard the noise of an approaching vehicle she automatically looked for a passing place. There was an entrance ahead and she trotted Gold up to the old metal gate and waited. Suddenly, Jenna's heart started pounding. Moving slowly through the narrow, winding lane she caught sight of the top of Kerry's lorry coming towards them. If she stayed where she was,

Kerry could trap them in the entrance. If she went on down the road, Kerry might even drive into them if she was as angry now as she had been earlier. Jenna unlatched the gate and was grateful to the person who, many years before, had hung it so well that it still swung easily. Trotting past the faded sign hanging from it, she realized she was entering an abandoned airfield. Urging Gold into a canter, she heard a loud clanging bang behind her. Kerry had driven through the closing gate, forcing it open with her bumper. The track was surfaced with hard, gray tarmac polished over the years by tires and weather. Gold slipped and almost fell, but Jenna kicked him forward and he found his feet on grass. Kerry was almost upon them when the lane opened out into a huge, fenced field of concrete, lined with tall weeds that grew along the cracks. Here Kerry had the upper hand as her vehicle, though cumbersome, was designed for this uncompromising surface. Jenna was terrified. Gold couldn't gallop here – not without risking his precious limbs – not without slipping, falling, crashing, and crushing their bones on the unrelenting ground. She trotted as fast as she could, and Gold responded with a wonderful lengthening of his stride, but it wasn't enough to pull clear of the lorry. Jenna knew Kerry was playing with her as a cat plays with a mouse. Round and round the airfield she chased her, keeping just behind the anxious, lathered horse, blocking the exit and revving her engine to see if Jenna would fall when Gold shied. The "game" went on too long for Jenna but she didn't know how to finish it. All around them was a strong post and rail fence. She looked for gaps or weak places, wondering if she dared to jump it, but she was getting tired and Gold was confused and excited by the strange behavior of the lorry. Then she saw it, one stretch of fence at the far side of the field with the top rail lowered. She had to try it, and she'd just have to pray that the landing would be safe. Kerry saw it too, and guessed what Jenna was planning. Gold's legs were aching from the pounding on the hard surface but he willingly listened to Jenna when she asked him to canter as they approached the fence. It was a reasonable height, and Gold quickened towards it in his usual exuberant jumping style, but Jenna checked him, concentrating hard on her approach, trying to push away the image of the lorry racing behind them. This was just another practice fence. She tried to forget she was riding bareback…she just sat and held him into the jump. For once Gold was easy, relaxed in his mouth, listening to Jenna. By the time they were close enough to see the huge, gaping ditch on the landing side of the fence it was too late. Jenna was committed to either jumping it or crashing into it, and Gold was too clever for the latter. He gathered himself up and flew. Jenna heard the sound of a car horn, the sickening crunch of tearing metal and shattering glass, the sweet thud of Gold's hooves as they struck into the soft, yielding grass and then she was falling,

114

rolling, curled into a ball in an attempt to protect herself. The long grasses held her, caught her, wrapped her, and she was still. Jenna's body was twisted and knotted in the grassy web. As she straightened herself out slowly she kept her eyes tight shut and waited, hoping against hope that it had all been a ghastly, horrible dream.

Chapter seven

Jenna knew it had all been a dream when she eventually opened her eyes and found Steve standing anxiously over her. She shut them again, nausea and dizziness sweeping over her. Steve was on his way to America, he was probably in the air at that very moment; she must have hit her head very badly to conjure him up from nowhere. She tried again, opening one eye at a time. He was still there.

"Jenna…are you all right, sweetheart?"

"No…are you in America?" she had to know.

Steve laughed, "I don't seem to be, do I?"

"I feel sick!" Jenna turned over and retched uncontrollably. Steve held her and soothed her with words until it had passed.

"You took quite a tumble…Gold made an amazing effort over that ditch, I bet you'd have stayed on if you'd had a saddle."

"Were you watching then?" Jenna was surprised. She could remember everything that had happened, but her sense of time had gone haywire, she couldn't work out whether minutes or hours had gone past since her fall.

"I was, it was one of the worst moments of my life. I was driving full tilt across the airfield, powerless to do anything except sound my horn to try to stop you. All I succeeded in doing was crashing my car into the fence, trying to head Kerry away from you."

"She's mad," Jenna said quietly.

"I'm afraid she is," Steve agreed. "She's permanently on medication. She shouldn't be driving, she probably shouldn't even be allowed out by herself, but her parents can't keep her locked up, and when she took the lorry this morning they hadn't a clue where she'd gone with it...or why."

"But how come you're here?" Jenna was still not sure this wasn't a dream.

"We got a text message on the way to the airport from Kerry, saying that Rachel wasn't to worry because she had "taken care of you." It was really weird, "taken" was spelled in capital letters. I had no idea she even knew you, but Rachel was immediately suspicious – apparently Kerry has been saying odd things to Rachel and asking questions about you for some time. Then Rachel's mum called to ask if we knew anything about Kerry taking the lorry, and it all began to fall into place. We didn't know where you were, but Rachel got through to Kerry on her phone and made her tell us. Kerry said that the two of you had had an argument, and that you'd gone off by yourself across Castle Hills, but she was waiting to take you home. I drove like a maniac, I was caught by at least three speed cameras on the way but we still arrived too late."

"Only just a bit," said Jenna gratefully. Her head was beginning to pound and every bone in her body ached, but Steve was holding her very close to him... she thought it was probably worth it.

***

Over the next few days Jenna's bruises turned from black and blue to green and purple. Her ankle, where the dog had bitten her, swelled up and she had to have antibiotics, but there were no bones broken. All-in-all, she felt things could have been a lot worse. Gold was fine, Steve and Rachel had postponed their trip and Dave and Angie were in a quiet state of shock about what had happened, (worse still, what *might* have happened), to Jenna, alone out on the moors, pursued by a mad woman with a strange grudge.

Once or twice Jenna had been able to laugh about some aspects of her ordeal. Trust Jenna, Steve told her fondly, to find the only miniature poodle in an area populated by sheep dogs and terriers and get bitten by it. Mostly though, she was haunted by re-living her feelings of fear, loneliness, and confusion. Sleeping was a problem, because it was at night, alone in her bedroom, that her usual rational way of looking at things left her.

118

Kerry was in hospital, back at the psychiatric unit where she had spent many years of her troubled life.

One morning Rachel came to see Jenna at the hotel to try to explain her sister's actions. They sat in the lounge, drinking coffee. Jenna nibbled one of Angie's homemade biscuits and curled herself up into the cool, unyielding comfort of the deep leather armchair.

"I'm so, so sorry," Rachel began, "you wouldn't believe how awful I feel about what's happened."

Privately, Jenna thought she probably felt worse, but she kept this to herself.

"This isn't the first time Kerry's done something like this, she gets the wrong end of the stick."

"Wrong end of the stick?" Jenna exclaimed. "Is that what you call it?"

"It happens when she's been in hospital for a time, she can't accept that things have moved on for everyone else," Rachel told her, ignoring Jenna's outburst.

"She said you and Steve were getting married, and she accused me of messing it up for you...but that's not true, is it?"

"We were engaged, that bit's true, but that was nearly three years ago."

"Before I'd even met Steve?"

"Yes, Kerry is, as you know, very confused, very ill..."

"But how could she have thought all that? She didn't know me, I'd never seen her before." Jenna

119

was angry, wondering why she felt guilty for something she was sure she hadn't done.

Rachel took a deep breath, "I guess that was probably my fault. I told her about you once when I visited her, before she came out of hospital. It was a bit of a joke really, she asked about Steve, and I said he'd got himself a teenage girlfriend. He was always talking about you, how well you rode, how pretty you were. I really don't think he knew he was doing it."

Jenna's heart missed a beat when she heard this, and the ghost of a smile touched her lips.

"If I'm honest, I suppose I was a bit jealous, after all, there was a time, ages ago, when I thought we'd probably get married. We were teenage sweethearts, our families were good friends and it all seemed so perfect, but it didn't work out – we were probably too young. When we split up I was devastated. It was a bad time for me and I became anorexic and I even had a stupid attempt at killing myself...Oh, I made sure I was going to be found in time, but it shook everyone up, especially Kerry."

"How old were you?" Jenna suddenly found herself feeling some compassion for Rachel, the girl who seemed to have everything, except the boy she loved.

"I was 17, not much older than you, and we'd been going out for two years. It hurts when you're that age, you think things will last forever and when they don't, it's as if your whole world comes crashing down around you."

"But why does Kerry hate me so much?" Jenna asked.

"She doesn't hate you, it was what she thought you were doing that she hated. She hates anything she thinks will make me unhappy."

"But why?" For the first time in her life Jenna was beginning to think being an only child might be preferable after all.

"I'm not sure. I think it's because Kerry was ill so often when we were growing up, she started to live her life through me. She's never had a boyfriend of her own and I suppose being twins, we're a lot closer than ordinary sisters. She thinks she can never be happy, and she's come to accept that, but she can't bear it if I'm not happy."

Jenna sat in the big armchair and hugged her knees to her chest, trying to imagine living a life without any hope of happiness. Anyone could be sad sometimes, Jenna knew that of course. She got as anxious, grumpy and fed up as the next teenage girl, but Kerry's unhappiness sounded more complete, more utterly hopeless. The thought of it sent a shiver up her spine and she started to feel an understanding and even some forgiveness towards Rachel's sister that certainly wasn't there before. She still needed answers though.

"What did she think she was going to do to me when she took me out to the moors?"

Rachel took a deep breath, there were still a lot of things that Jenna didn't know.

"I'm afraid she's been doing things to you for some time. I didn't realize; it's only just fallen into place since I've talked to her about it. Apparently she just wanted to scare you at first, make you look like a silly little girl in front of Steve to put him off you. She's been putting whole oats into Gold's coarse mix to make him unrideable, and she says she made a few creepy phone calls too."

"It was her, was it?" Jenna felt as though she was nearing the completion of a jigsaw and had just found a lost piece under the couch. "I bet she sent that card too...and the flowers."

"Probably, the trouble was, her plan to make you look silly backfired, because you were quite capable of handling Gold even when he was over-topped on oats; if anything, she could see that Steve was even more impressed. So she decided to stop you from riding for a while. She waited outside your room, followed you to the stairs…"

"Alice!" Jenna exclaimed, "she'd been to my room to get a book when she had her accident, she insisted she'd been pushed, but of course no one wanted to believe her. And it must have been Kerry who almost knocked me over when I was picking the holly."

Rachel nodded sadly, "Kerry has admitted she spent quite a bit of time hanging around the hotel at Christmas, just watching everyone; she said she was hoping to see me and Steve together."

"Did she dress up in a cloak?" Jenna asked, though she already knew the answer.

"Yes, she realized how easy it would be to get away with creeping around if she looked as though she was part of the cast," said Rachel. "I think she quite enjoyed fooling everyone."

"But I still don't understand how she came to be picking me up, I got the horsebox hire number from a card in the tackroom, how come it was Kerry?"

"Apparently that was sheer coincidence. Mum and dad hire the lorry out, dad does a bit of driving as a sideline, and it just happened that Kerry answered the phone when you called. I don't suppose she could believe her luck when she realized it was you calling. She said she only meant to talk to you and scare you off, but things got out of hand...she always did have a bit of a temper."

"You can say that again," said Jenna with feeling.

"Anyway," Rachel said quietly, "I hope you can forgive Kerry.... and me too for that matter."

Jenna thought about this for a few moments and found that she no longer felt anger towards the strange, sad girl who had frightened her so badly. But what did she feel? Hatred? Fear? Compassion even? Not really, she thought. The best way to describe it was numbness. She found she had no feelings for Kerry, nor for her sister Rachel, who was, after all, still whisking Steve off to America just when she needed him to help her with Gold's show jumping. Jenna smiled a small, inward smile when she realized what she had just admitted to herself. She was jealous of Rachel, horribly jealous. She was jealous of her superiority, her confidence, her experience, her maturity, her good looks, her spectacular figure, her expensive wardrobe...anything else? Well, that would do for a start, Jenna told herself, but what did she have that Rachel didn't? It did look rather as though she might have Steve, not yet, not now, but one day, and Jenna was more than prepared to wait. Years would probably have to pass, but while she was waiting, perhaps she and James could be more than just friends. The more she thought about it the more she liked the idea, she just hoped she hadn't left it too late.

Rachel looked at Jenna properly for the first time. There seemed to be a strange, small smile playing over her pretty lips, and Rachel saw how beautiful she was going to be, and hoped Steve wouldn't break Jenna's heart. Then a crazy thought crossed through her head and made her smile too. Look out Steve, it might be your heart that gets broken this time, she silently warned him.

***

After several days of solid rain, Jenna felt they'd earned the crisp, bright weather that followed. It wasn't cold considering it was January and, down at the stables, Jenna worked in her shirtsleeves, mucking out the loose boxes and sweeping the yard. She had replaced the bin full of oat enriched coarse mix with a less heating batch and the effect had been calming not just on Gold, but on Tufty too.

"You see," she'd explained to her dad, who'd been none too happy about throwing out a bin full of good food, "Tufty was getting his rations from the same bin and the thinner he got the more I gave him. And, the more oats he ate the more excited he got, which made him even thinner…see what I mean?"

"Not really," said Dave, thoroughly confused.

"Well, for a pony like Tufty, too much rich food just made him silly. He burned up more energy leaping and fretting away, pawing the floor of his stable, and digging holes in it. What he needs is a less heating, more fattening type of mix, a special one for older ponies," Jenna explained.

"That sounds expensive," Dave said doubtfully.

"He's worth it," Jenna reassured her father, "and it's much cheaper than having a new stable floor laid down."

She swept a last stray wisp of hay into a corner and went to saddle Gold, eager to be riding on such a fine day. She'd schooled him once since her adventure with Kerry and he'd been awful, but Jenna had blamed the weather and was optimistic today. She still carried the memory of his wonderful behavior when she'd ridden him bit-less and bareback across the wild, moorland country. But that seemed a long time ago and there were just three more days before the show. Jenna knew she needed every minute left to her to prepare.

The ground in the paddock was greasy and muddy underfoot, but Gold didn't mind. He eyed up the fences Jenna had put up for him to jump and a quiver of excitement went through him. He loved to jump almost as much as he had loved to race. Their warm-up work was not good. Gold wouldn't round his back, and Jenna felt useless and couldn't help pulling at him roughly in an attempt to make him drop his head and accept her hands.

"Oh, let's just jump," she growled, turning towards the first fence in her course.

Gold flew. He took charge and galloped. Jenna steered him, just about, but as each small fence flashed beneath her she knew they were only clearing them by sheer luck; if the fences had been bigger, things would have been very different.

"Isn't he going a bit fast, dear?" The sunshine had tempted Angie from the busy kitchen and given her the idea of coming to watch her daughter ride.

Jenna pulled up and came over to her mum.

"Is it that obvious?" she asked.

"Well, you know I'm not an expert, but it did look a bit scary around the corners. Were you practicing going against the clock?"

This made Jenna laugh. "No, Mum," she said affectionately. "He's always like this, it's as if he is running away from something but he seems to love jumping so it can't be that."

"And yet you told us he was so well behaved the other day, and you didn't even have a bridle then. Perhaps it's the bit he objects to. I know I would, I can't imagine how any horse puts up with that great lump of nasty, cold metal in their mouth…Jenna! Hang on a minute darling, where are you going? Jenna, I haven't got long, I'm needed for the lunches."

Angie was astonished to find herself holding Gold's reins that Jenna had just pushed into her hands before sprinting back in the direction of the stables. A few minutes passed and Angie nervously patted Gold's cheek, carefully keeping her fingers well away from his mouth.

"I'm sure you're a very nice horse who wouldn't dream of biting me," she told him as Jenna returned out of breath and carrying a headcollar.

"I'm going to take his bridle off and try him in this instead," she explained, buckling reins to the D rings at each side and tightening the noseband a little.

Jenna wasn't really worried when she put her foot in the stirrup and stepped back up on to Gold. Somehow, she already knew what would happen, but she still asked Angie to stay for a minute.

"Just in case you need to call an ambulance," she told her anxious mother.

"Oh, be careful, darling…oh, I wish I'd never said anything now."

Gold tested the contact by lowering his head, feeling for the hard, cold metal he hated so much. He was ready to do battle with it, but finding nothing there he had no need to fight. This was how he wanted to be ridden, but how could he have told

Jenna that his mouth was unusually short, his tongue a little too large and, that any bit, though not actually painful, was just never going to be comfortable. Gold had never understood why he should have to put up with it…perhaps at last he wasn't going to have to. Jenna wrapped her legs around her horse, sat tall, and asked him to trot. Gold responded with a round, supple back. He dropped his head and resisted the desire to race towards the fence. There was no need, he wasn't trying to get away from the bit, there was no bit. Jump after jump came and went and, although turning without a proper bridle wasn't easy, there was none of the panic and dash of before. Jenna felt the tears pricking behind her eyes and soon they were streaming down her face. All she could do when she got down from her precious, glorious horse was to sob into his mane and stroke his damp neck over and over again.

Chapter eight

Jenna stood by the ringside and waited for her number to be called. For the very first time she was nervous, mind numbingly nervous. She was experiencing an almost paralyzing fear. Her mouth was dry, her palms damp, her muscles limp, and if anyone had asked her her name, she probably wouldn't have known it. It was odd how it had hit her so suddenly; she'd felt fine at breakfast, so excited when the lorry came, and warming up had been a picnic. She'd managed to walk the show jumping course with perfect concentration, carefully considering every turn and approach. It was as if she had been moving through a dream that had suddenly turned into a nightmare when the full realization of what she was about to do hit her.

"You're in next, love." The ring steward smiled at her, noticing her faraway expression. "Hello, is there anybody in there?" he cooed.

"What? Me? Oh, I'm sorry, I was miles away,"

Jenna stammered, gathering her woolly thoughts to-gether.

"I could see that! I was just saying you are the next to jump, after the bay horse."

"Thank you," Jenna muttered.

She gathered up her reins and walked Gold round in a small circle, her legs nudging him forward, waking him up, and telling him that something was about to happen. He dropped his head happily into his bridle, liking the bit-less hackamore that Jenna had bought him. This worked with a lever action on his jaw and his poll, the long metal cheek pieces curled down below his mouth and a short, bright curb chain nestled into his chin groove. This would tighten quickly if he fought with Jenna's hands, but it was so comfortable he found he didn't want to. Jenna heard the sound of the big school doors being dragged open, and she knew that her turn had really come. As she crossed the threshold into the brightly lit indoor arena, she felt her worries lift and her head clear. She knew exactly what she had to do. It was as if she had been riding in competitions all her life and, when the bell went off, she cantered towards the first fence. It was very far from being a perfect round but to James, watching nervously from the gallery, she and Gold looked exquisite; a pretty girl on a pretty horse, he thought to himself and he felt proud he was with them. To Jenna the round seemed to pass in the blink of an eye. As each fence came to them, Gold picked up and jumped, he didn't rush and he didn't pull, no poles fell, and there was a smattering of appreciative applause from the small, cold crowd who had turned up to watch.

"Clear round!" the commentator's muffled voice boomed from the speaker.

James had got up before daybreak and driven for two hours to be there in time to watch her ride. He'd been tired and hungry, cold and anxious as he sat in the gallery and waited for her turn to jump, but now all that was forgotten and he raced over to meet her as she rode up the tunnel towards the lorry park. Jenna jumped down from Gold and passed his reins to James as she peeled off her sticky, sweaty gloves.

"That was brilliant," he told her, breathless with running, "and there haven't been many clear rounds so far."

"It's a pity it was just the warm-up competition, I just hope he goes as well in the Talent Spotters this afternoon." Jenna grinned at him, delighted now that it was over. "Wasn't he great though? So different from the awful rounds we did at Trent Hall when I couldn't stop him. I wish we'd thought of trying a hackamore ages ago. It just felt so amazing being able to control him for once!"

"Come, on put the golden horse back in the lorry, and I'll buy you breakfast," James teased her, and he dared to take her by the hand as he led them both away.

Sitting at a coffee stained table a few minutes later, drinking Coke from the can, Jenna allowed James to hold her hand again as it rested across the plastic table cloth. Or rather, she was so deep in thought, reliving Gold's round, that she didn't really notice, which wasn't quite the same thing, but it was good enough for James.

"It's really kind of you to come all this way to help me," she told him, suddenly noticing that he was staring rather helplessly into her eyes. She took back her hand to scratch her nose but gave it back to him afterwards, because she decided she rather liked it. James was a very handsome young man, and he had already attracted some admiring glances from a tall blonde girl sitting with her friend at the next table.

"It's no trouble," he reassured her, "I'm enjoying myself. I'd only be studying if I weren't here. Oh, and thanks for phoning me the other day...it was really nice to hear from you."

James didn't tell Jenna that after an hour chatting to her on the phone, he had gone around the house singing at the top of his voice until Alice had shouted at him to shut up and threatened to thump him with her crutch.

Jenna risked glancing at the blonde and was, rather perversely, annoyed to see that she'd turned her attentions to two boys at another table. The canteen was bustling with young riders. The most experienced sat relaxed and chatting, wearing casual, bright-colored jackets over their smart, dark riding coats; others ate silently with their parents, forcing every nervous mouthful down, mindful of sauce stains on their smart clothes. The noise levels were high and the strip lighting intense and glaring, making Jenna want to escape to the cold, subdued daylight outside.

"Soon be time for the jump off," she told James, and they left the cafe together, James with his arm around Jenna's waist, thinking he was probably the luckiest guy in the world.

Jenna wasn't nervous for the jump off. She just went in and did her job neatly, correctly, and without fuss. Gold jumped for the fun of it and, because Jenna got him to each fence on exactly the right stride for him to jump it, his confidence in her grew. They were not the fastest in the class, but their time was good enough to earn them third place and a frothy yellow rosette with long tails where the name of the class sponsor was printed in gold.

Jenna accepted the rosette in a bit of a dream, and as she cantered round the arena with the other winners, she wore a huge grin across her face. She thought her heart might burst with pride in Gold, whose extravagant paces were causing some admiring looks from the ringside. She leaned forward and smoothed his warm neck. How she wished her mum and dad had been there to see her do well. Steve too, she knew he would be thrilled when she texted him later. Steve was racing again today, his trip to

America postponed until the end of the week. Jenna knew that Rachel had gone racing with him but, to her surprise, this had only caused her the slightest twinge of jealousy. She was trying hard not to mind about Steve and made herself think about James instead. It was definitely getting easier, and James was gorgeous – he was helping her to forget.

The course for the long awaited Talent Spotters competition was considerably bigger than the warm-up class. When Jenna went in to walk it, she was overwhelmed. Then she remembered a tip Steve had once given her and decided to tag along behind a very knowledgeable looking man who was giving advice to his daughter, a thin, pale girl with protruding teeth which were covered in wire. Listening hard, while trying to pretend she wasn't, Jenna stayed close to her unwitting mentor and got some clues as to how to ride the tricky, up-to-height course. The man turned and winked at her as they left the arena.

"Good luck love, don't forget to steady up for the gate," he grinned, and Jenna blushed to the roots of her hair, but grinned back.

At the lorry, James had tacked up Gold, oiled his hooves and put on some smart white tendon boots that he'd brought as a surprise for Jenna.

"He looks wonderful in them," Jenna said with delight.

"Alice sent them, she won't be needing them for a while, and she thought you'd find them useful today. I hope they're going to be lucky for you," James told her as he legged her up into the saddle. For a moment, Jenna could hardly believe she was really there, really about to jump her own, precious, talented horse.

And I might even manage to stay in control for once, she thought to herself.

The atmosphere inside the warm-up arena was tense and serious as professional looking young jockeys and immaculately turned out horses cantered slow circles. There were anxious parents and trainers amongst the audience watching from the ringside, some words of advice were spoken, but mostly there was just the solid sound of hoof beats on the tan, and the occasional thud of a falling pole. Jenna joined them, working Gold slowly at first, flexing his neck to the left and to the right, and suppling his back with the simple, stretching exercises Steve had taught her. When they came to canter, Gold forgot himself for a second and he rushed forward, only to be caught by the pressure of the hackamore, which he did not resent. Jenna sat tall and proud and jumped both practice fences three times before she was satisfied.

Five minutes later they were walking into the ring. Gold looked at everything, his eyes on stalks as he caught the electric atmosphere that filled the arena. He jogged sideways and kicked over a plant pot, and Jenna was relieved when the bell went and she was able to start. This was the biggest course of fences

135

Gold had ever jumped and it was technical too, with some of the distances between the obstacles set long or short to catch the riders. The boldness and brightness of the decorated jumps made Gold back off a little on take-off and Jenna found herself having to ride him strongly forward instead of holding him back. The course suited both of them, jump after jump seemed to meet them just right and not one pole did Gold touch. To Jenna the whole round had a dream-like quality, she rode by instinct, her body and her brain perfectly in tune with Gold. There was a loud, triumphant whistle from James as she rode out which snapped her from her trance.

"Brilliant!" James was by her side, taking Gold's reins from Jenna's trembling hands. "You rode that so well. There was a couple sitting next to me and they couldn't stop saying nice things about you."

"He was amazing! We just seemed to be flying and he did everything I asked." Jenna felt near to tears, but she didn't know why.

"Are you going to go for it in the jump off?" James asked her.

"There's another round to go first, and only double clears go through to the jump off. But apparently they build the course so big that sometimes there aren't any double clears," Jenna explained.

"Well, there've only been six clear rounds so far, so you must be in with a chance," James told her.

The next round was bigger still and the course now included a narrow stile and a treble, a line of three

136

big fences in a row. To Gold, who had been trained over huge steeplechase fences, height and width held no fears, but he was unused to approaching so many obstacles in such a short space of time. He had to put his trust in Jenna who rode him so naturally. At each fence she saw a good stride and Gold met every one perfectly. They had only one nasty moment at the stile, a set of narrow, white rails that loomed tall and had to be jumped in exactly the right place to leave them up. Jenna rode for the very center but Gold had never seen a jump so compressed and contained before and approached it very cautiously. Just two strides from take off he'd lost so much impulsion that Jenna thought he was going to stop, but her riding school days came back to her, and she shouted at him and kicked him sharply forward, bullying him into the air and safely over. There was a cheer from the gallery, which was full of people who had appeared to watch the climax of this prestigious class.

"That's our first double clear!" The sweet words of the commentator rang in her ears. "Jenna Wells and Gold are our current leaders."

"The first of many, I expect," she told James who had whisked her up into the air in a big hug as soon as her feet touched the ground.

"I didn't want to tell you before in case it put you off, but that course was causing loads of problems. The rider before you had twenty faults!"

"Well, I'm not going to jump off, I decided when I was in there. He's not ready to jump that height at speed, I've only just got him to calm down." Jenna was firm and quite sure she was doing the right thing.

James looked disappointed.

"But if there are other clears and you don't jump off, then you won't win the training you've been going on about. I thought that was the whole reason for entering this class."

"It was, but I just know Gold isn't ready. Rushing him at this stage might put him back at square one. And if we don't go for it, then there really isn't any point in making him jump again when he's just done such a lovely round for me."

"I suppose so." James had wanted her to win so badly, and he couldn't keep the disappointment from his voice. "Let's go and untack him then."

Back at the lorry, Henry Pearce, the driver, was just emerging from his cab, rubbing sleep from his eyes and yawning loudly.

"Are you ready for home?" he asked Jenna. "And have you been doing well?"

"Yes, and yes," she laughed, liking this plump, quiet man and comparing him fleetingly to the last person who had taken her and Gold for a ride in their lorry.

"She was a superstar," said James loyally.

"Gold was the superstar," Jenna told them, quietly stroking his dear face, smoothing her hands over his clean, white blaze that grew crookedly down his nose and was little more than an elongated star.

"James, can you go and tell them I'm not jumping off while I get Gold untacked?"

James went and Jenna set about removing Gold's boots and taking the studs from his shoes. Only minutes had passed when she heard the sound of running feet and James was back.

"You've won! You've won!" he shouted breathlessly. Yours was the only clear round! Come on, they're calling for you."

Gold wasn't used to such rough treatment, and he put his ears back and snapped at Henry when he pulled up his girth so quickly it pinched his skin. James threw Jenna up into the saddle so ferociously she very nearly left it again over the other side. With her hat unfastened, still buttoning her coat, she was flustered and astonished and sure she must be dreaming.

As her official chaperone, James felt he had every right to go into the arena with Jenna and stood by her proudly while the class sponsors, who owned a large garage, presented Jenna with a flowing red rosette and an envelope containing the details of her training course. Then she had to lead the lap of honor round the ring and the rosette flew off Gold's bridle and she dropped the envelope, but James was there to retrieve them.

Jenna jumped down into his arms.

"You clever, clever thing," he kept saying over and over as he hugged her tightly to him, never wanting to let her go.

Jenna hugged him back and enjoyed his words and suddenly his belief in her seemed the most important thing in the world.

"You are so nice," she whispered so that he could hear, but under her breath she added "too nice really, much nicer than me."

But James was so much in love at that moment that he wouldn't have cared even if he had heard her.

Steve's race meeting had finished early, and he'd sent his horses home with Rachel in his father's lorry and driven his car like a maniac to be in time to watch Jenna ride. He'd sat at the back of the gallery and seen her second round and led the cheering, jumping from his seat as she cleared the final fence. He watched the rest of the competition and knew before she did that she had won the class; on a whim he'd rushed off to the nearest garage and bought all the overpriced carnations he could carry and waited to surprise her when she'd finished her lap of honor.

He saw her come out of the arena, her face sparkling, almost dazed, and something stopped him coming forward. He hesitated, then stepped back to watch, half hidden by people and horses, as she jumped down and embraced James for what seemed to him like a very, very long time.

He looked at the flowers in his arms.

'What am I doing?' he asked himself. 'She's just a

kid, what's she going to think if I give her these? She's got James, and she doesn't need me.'

Turning away, he put the flowers into the hands of a bewildered, gray haired lady and left the showground with a strange choking pain in the back of his throat.

Chapter nine

Jenna knew that winning the Talent Spotters Competition was the first really cool thing she'd ever done. She wasn't the greatest student at school, due entirely to a lack of interest in the things she was taught, but horses she adored and they were something she had always known she could be good at…perhaps very good. The days following the competition passed in a daze; she wore a permanent smile and kept forgetting to do things because she was reliving the moments over and over again in her head. She had made page five of the local paper, a rather blurry photo of her with her hat slipping over one eye and wearing a silly grin, but Gold looked stunning, so she didn't mind too much. Underneath the picture it said "Promising young show jumper, Jenny Wills, one to watch for the future," which was flattering, but not very accurate.

James was on the phone every day, and he texted her little messages almost every hour, not all of which she replied to. She saw almost nothing of Steve, whose horses were still stabled at his father's in readiness for his trip to America. He sent her a card to congratulate her for winning the Talent Spotters Competition, but the words were so distant and formal it left Jenna wondering what she'd done to offend him.

Two weeks after the show, Jenna received the phone call which she'd been waiting for, inviting her to attend a training day in February at the home of show jumper Harry Houseman, the youngest of the three famous Houseman brothers. If Jenna had been in the habit of having posters of young men on her bedroom wall, (which she wasn't, being too old for such things), Harry would certainly have been there.

Glowing with excitement, Jenna went in search of her mother to tell her the exciting news. She found her in the kitchen, (where else? she thought to herself,) sharing a plate of homemade biscuits with Mr. Penrose.

"Your mum's been telling me about your murder mystery shenanigans. I'm glad it went well, Jenna," he said to her. "Not that I agree with dragging up the past like that, but I'm glad it was a success, it's good for the hotel."

"Oh, yes thanks, it did. The steeplechase was fun too." she looked at him slyly, remembering how he'd warned her against riding in it.

"You stayed on then?" He asked her equally slyly, and Jenna wondered how much he knew.

"And we didn't raise any ghosts by doing it, despite what James thought at one point," said Jenna, deliberately avoiding his question.

"I know what you're getting at, young lady. I know I said no good would come of it…but perhaps I was wrong…all right, obviously I was wrong – I have been known to be wrong before!"

Jenna laughed, Mr. Penrose didn't often admit to being wrong. She took a biscuit from the plate and nibbled it thoughtfully.

"It seems ages ago now, lots of things have happened since then," Jenna told him, itching to mention her news.

"So I see, got your picture in the paper, no less! Well, I'm very proud of you bringing a bit of fame to our village, we'll be seeing you on the *Horse of the Year Show* next." Mr. Penrose was laughing at her, but not unkindly.

Jenna blushed, she wasn't used to being the target of such praise.

"How's Tufty? You haven't brought him to see me recently."

"He's fine now, getting fatter. You've just reminded me, I've got to do a proper job of mucking out his box this morning," Jenna told him, suddenly feeling guilty for skimping it for the past few days.

"You run along and do it, can't have you neglecting my old favorite," Mr. Penrose said.

She decided she would tell her mum about Harry Houseman later.

"Don't forget James is coming over soon," Angie called after her as she left.

"As if I could forget a thing like that," said Jenna, pleased at the little thrill of pleasure that now arrived, unasked for, when she heard James' name.

Tufty was standing by the paddock gate as she passed, but he wasn't asking to come in. He was just resting, drifting into sleep and dreaming, his old head nodding slightly, peaceful and serene. His new food had brought about a dramatic change in him, and he had returned to living out his old age with tranquility replacing the exhausting, driving energy that had tormented him. Jenna stopped to stare at him, and Tufty hardly noticed.

"You just stay there and sleep," she told him, "and I'll work myself to a frazzle on your behalf."

She got her fork, a shovel, and the wheelbarrow and set about the hot work of lifting and digging, shifting, and sweeping. When the floor was cleanly swept Jenna dragged a bale of straw from the feed store and used her pocketknife to cut the taught strings. They separated with a satisfying thud, releasing the tightly bound, yellow stalks. Near the door she stooped to examine the damage Tufty had done to the ancient brick floor with his unceasing pawing when Kerry had been messing with his feed. He'd made quite a hole and a brick had lifted and been kicked to one side. Finding it, Jenna scraped dirt from the hole with a stick before replacing it. To her surprise, instead of earth at the bottom, there seemed to be some metal there. Carefully, she moved the brick next to it and now she could see what it was. Working with her fingertips she scraped and scratched away at the grime until she had loosened the little metal box and was holding it gingerly in her hands.

Jenna wasn't sure what she was frightened of, but the burning desire to know what was inside the box was almost equaled by her fear of it. She sat there, balanced on her heels for a very long time, not moving, hardly breathing, feeling the surprising weight of the little black box in her grubby fingers. Then she stood up and carried it to the table in the tack room where she stared at it again. Eventually her curiosity got the better of her. Using her pocketknife, she worked away at the rust that sealed the lid to its base. There was a loud snap as the hinges broke, and inside was a package of oiled cloth, stained and bulky, but soft and tinder dry. Reverently, terrified of what she might find, Jenna unraveled the length of fabric until it released its secret to her astonished eyes. She found herself holding a small pistol; its bone handle was pale and mottled and the barrel gleamed dully in the light filtering through the dirty window. Jenna turned it over, looking with wonderment at her unexpected treasure.

"Jenna," James called to her from outside, breaking the little spell the tiny gun had had over her.

"I'm in the tack room," she called back.

James sauntered in through the door, smiling and looking very smart in new, pale gray trousers.

"Look what I've found. Do you think it might be Abram's?" Jenna asked.

She went to pass it to James, handle first in the polite way one might offer some scissors.

"Jenna!" James' voice was just a whisper, the color had drained from his face. "Jenna, just put it down, very slowly on the table. No! Don't point it at yourself. Didn't you notice that the hammer's cocked?"

"Is it?" said Jenna innocently, "is that bad then?"

"Jenna, that gun is cocked, it might be loaded and it could go off at any..."

The shock of the explosion left them cowering on the floor. Jenna was aware of a searing, burning pain in her hand and of glass raining down on them. For a while they both kept still, stunned by the noise, huddled together in the dirt, watching the dust and flakes of ancient plaster settle all around them.

"Are you all right?" Jenna asked at last.

"Yes, a bit scratched, that's all, what about you?"

Jenna couldn't answer. The gun had gone off in her hand, the pain was bad enough but the thought of what she might have done to herself was sickening. Slowly, she forced herself to look. Her hand was red and bleeding, blackened with soot, but her fingers were there, and she wriggled them gratefully.

"My hand is a bit burned but there's nothing broken...or missing." The relief was evident in her voice.

"Which is more than can be said for the window, there's glass everywhere."

James helped her carefully to her feet and winced when he saw her poor, damaged hand.

"The gun must have been Abram's," said Jenna with wonder in her voice, "it must have lain there for all those years, undisturbed until Tufty practically dug it up. It's a blessing it didn't go off in his stable – with his nerves like they were, he'd probably have died on the spot."

James found this image rather funny but hated himself for it and knowing Jenna wouldn't appreciate it, he kept his thoughts to himself. Jenna was still deep in thought and luckily hadn't noticed the fleeting smile that passed over James' dusty face.

"But why hide it there?" she asked. "It wasn't exactly easy to get at. Anyway, if Abram did hide it there, why couldn't he find it when he was called for trial? He might have gotten off if he could prove where his gun was."

"Perhaps someone else moved it, hid it there, just so he couldn't find it. Someone who wanted to make it look as though Abram had killed Arnold, someone who wanted both brothers out of the way..."

"Cressida?" They both said her name at the same time.

"Or Frederick Walton? Perhaps he wanted Cressida and the Green Horse."

"We'll never really know, of course, not for sure," said James reasonably. "Anyway, we'd better get your hand looked at. Here we are chatting about something that may or may not have happened years ago, and you're dripping blood all over my new trousers."

Suddenly Jenna burst out laughing.

"It's not funny, Mum will go mad when she sees them."

"I'm not laughing at that, I've just thought about Mr. Penrose. Only an hour ago I actually got him to admit he was wrong and that there was nothing to fear about messing about with ghosts from the past…he's going to be impossible now!"